ALEX LONDON

THE PRINCESS PROTECTION PROGRAM
AFTER EVER AFTER

🕮 GREENWILLOW BOOKS
An Imprint of HarperCollinsPublishers

The Princess Protection Program #2: After Ever After
Text copyright © 2025 by Charles Alexander London
Illustrations copyright © 2025 by James Firnhaber

All rights reserved. Manufactured in Harrisonburg, VA, United States of America. No part of this book may be used or reproduced in any manner whatsoever without written permission except in the case of brief quotations embodied in critical articles and reviews. For information address HarperCollins Children's Books, a division of HarperCollins Publishers, 195 Broadway, New York, NY 10007.
www.harpercollinschildrens.com

The text of this book is set in Tiempos Text.
Book design by Sylvie Le Floc'h

Library of Congress Cataloging-in-Publication Data
Names: London, Alex, author. | Firnhaber, James, illustrator.
Title: After ever after / by Alex London ; [illustrations by James Firnhaber].
Description: First edition. | New York, NY : Greenwillow Books, an imprint of HarperCollins Publishers, 2025. | Series: The Princess Protection Program ; #2 | Audience term: Preteens | Audience: Ages 8–12. | Audience: Grades 2–3. | Summary: Princess Rana, a fairy tale escapee embracing her new life at the Home Educational Academy, must return to her story to stop a shadowy monster and save her friends after dozens of frog princes and a dangerous threat appear at the academy.
Identifiers: LCCN 2024033425 (print) | LCCN 2024033426 (ebook) | ISBN 9780063303928 (hardcover) | ISBN 9780063303942 (ebook)
Subjects: CYAC: Fantasy. | Princesses—Fiction. | Characters in literature—Fiction. | LCGFT: Fantasy fiction. | Novels.
Classification: LCC PZ7.L84188 Af 2025 (print) | LCC PZ7.L84188 (ebook) | DDC [Fic]—dc23
LC record available at https://lccn.loc.gov/2024033425
LC ebook record available at https://lccn.loc.gov/2024033426

---

24 25 26 27 28 LBC 5 4 3 2 1
First Edition
Greenwillow Books

*For Maddie, of course,
whose story has only just begun*

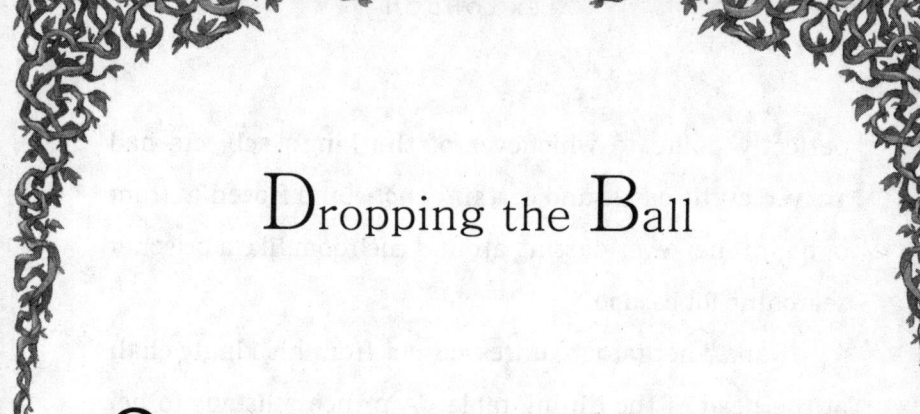

Dropping the Ball

Once upon a time, a princess jumped up from the dinner table.

Princess Rana, the only daughter of a prosperous king and queen, knew better than to jump up from the dinner table, but she'd been terribly startled by a knock at the castle door.

"My dear, it is unseemly for a princess to startle. Please sit down," said her mother, the queen, who had a long list of rules for how a princess should behave, which included no startling, no jumping, no leaping or laughing too loud. A princess also did not gasp, gape, giggle, or grunt. She did not burp, belch, bellow, or break wind.

There were other rules for Princess Rana to obey—too many to list in a book anyone would want to read.

Right now, the most relevant rule was that she sit at the dinner table and eat from her golden plate and remain perfectly polite to whichever of the king's subjects had arrived at the castle and certainly *not* stand frozen in front of her dinner, eyes darting around the room like a prisoner searching for escape.

"Rana," her father addressed her from his kingly chair at the head of the dining table. "A princess listens to her mother." He gestured back at her seat.

But Princess Rana stood, fear drowning her father's words. She listened for the footsteps of the servant who had come to announce the evening's unexpected visitor, though she knew, before the dining room doors even opened, who it would be.

"Your Majesties!" the servant announced. "May I present . . . a frog."

Into the dining room hopped a greenish-brownish, lumpy, bumpy frog, wet with well water and weary from travel.

Rana's heart sank. She'd run *away* from this frog only a few hours earlier.

"My princess!" he cried as he hopped into the room. "You left so quickly, I could not keep up on my little legs."

"You know this frog?" her mother asked.

"Of course she knows me!" said the frog. "I fetched the golden ball she dropped into a well in the woods. In exchange she promised I could come to her home and eat from her golden plate and sleep on her satin pillow!"

At this point, Princess Rana had turned beet red, shame having replaced fear.

Her mother gasped.

"You *spoke* with this frog?" her father groused. Her parents had strict rules about only speaking to members of the royal family.

"You dropped your ball into a *well*?" her mother lamented.

Her parents had strict rules about avoiding wells, which could splash water onto Rana's perfect gowns.

"You were in the *woods!*" both her parents cried out together. They had extremely strict rules about never going into the woods.

This rule was, perhaps, the wisest, as nothing good ever happens to a princess in any sort of woods in any sort of tale. Princesses who went into woods always came out changed.

Which was, of course, the whole point of going into those woods in the first place. Rana had *wanted* to change.

She was tired of being perfect all the time, tired of having neither friends nor fun, and most of all, tired of *rules*.

She'd gone into the woods precisely because she was not supposed to. She'd brought her ball precisely because she was not supposed to. And she'd dropped it into the well precisely because . . . well . . . that *had* been an accident.

But this frog had popped out and offered to help. Having never spoken to a frog before, she found it rather interesting, so she agreed, even though he was kind of gross looking and kind of weird sounding.

The problem was, he only offered to help her get her ball back if she agreed to let him come to the castle and eat off her plate and sleep on her pillow.

That seemed rather a lot to ask for, but she *did* want to get her ball back. She couldn't exactly ask her parents for a new one, not without explaining all the rules she'd broken to lose it in the first place.

So she'd agreed to the frog's terms, with no intention of keeping her end of the bargain. She was a princess and he was a frog, after all, and if she was willing to defy the king and queen from time to time, she could defy a frog this one time.

Once she had her ball back in her hand, she bolted. It was not the honorable thing to do, but it was effective.

"A deal's a deal," the frog told her parents. "I followed her from the well in the woods across the flowered meadows and all the way to the castle door. I have more than earned my dinner."

"Is this so?" Rana's father asked her.

Princess Rana, abashed, nodded.

Her father sighed and ordered the frog be allowed at the table. "A princess always keeps her word," he said. "That is an ironclad rule."

With that, the frog hopped onto the table and sat right beside Princess Rana's golden plate. Its tongue flicked out to eat her food.

The princess lost her appetite and asked to be excused.

The frog followed her, though again she objected.

"You promised him, did you not?" said her father.

"I did," she admitted.

"Rules are rules," said her mother.

"I am quite looking forward to a nice warm bed after sleeping so long in that cold wet well," croaked the frog.

"But you're a frog!" complained the princess, who didn't

think she was being unreasonable.

She could not be expected to let some frog into her private bedroom. There *had* to be a rule against that.

What good are rules if they won't protect me from unrelenting frogs? she wondered.

The frog was unfazed by her reluctance, or simply didn't care, and hopped right onto her pillow. "I don't take up much room," he told her. "And I don't snore . . . much."

"You cannot sleep in my bed," she said firmly.

"Of course not," the frog agreed. "Not without a bedtime story first. Read to me?"

"You pushy little lump!" she yelled at the frog, and snatched it up from her pillow. She held the warty thing up to her face so closely she could kiss it.

"That's no way for a princess to speak," said the frog.

"Go suck on a fly's nose!" She tossed the frog with all her might straight at the wall.

"Ah!" The frog flew end over end through the air. It hit the stone wall with a wet thump and then, before Rana's eyes, transformed from an unsightly frog into a prince. A handsome prince, slumped sideways on her bedroom floor.

"Princess!" he cried out from the ground, his voice silken

smooth where once it had been coarse and crude. "You've saved me! Now we can get married and live happily ever after! The witch's curse will be forever broken and I'll never have to be a frog again! Heinrich, ready the royal carriage!"

Rana clenched her jaw in anger.

Marriage was *never* a part of her promise. She knew that there were rules in her kingdom for princesses, and even more for wives, and if she'd had enough of the former, she wanted none of the latter.

"I am not going to marry you," she told him.

"Well, of course not!" agreed the frog prince. "Not until my servant fetches the carriage to bring you home! Heinrich!" He shouted down from her bedroom window. Was his servant somehow waiting outside? "It's me! I've returned! I've found a bride!"

How did Heinrich get here? she wondered.

Rana crept to the edge of her bedroom. Then crept into the hallway. Then she turned around and ran as fast as she could.

She fled down the stairs, past her parents in the dining room, out the door, and past the frog prince's devoted servant, Heinrich, a boy about the prince's age, who'd been waiting eagerly for his beloved prince's return.

"Wait!" called the servant. "Where is my prince? You aren't supposed to leave without him! If you do, he'll turn back into a—"

But the princess kept running, back to the woods.

Behind her, the cries of the prince and his servant rang in her ears. "Wait!" they called. "The curse isn't broken! This isn't how our story goes at all! Come back! Ribbit!"

But it was too late. The prince had turned back into a frog.

The servant cried out in woe and agony, but Princess Rana wasn't around to hear any of it. She had run right out of her story, breaking the most important rule a princess must follow. She ditched her kingdom and meant never to return. She didn't want to be a princess anymore.

CHAPTER ONE

Homework Cookies

Rana woke up with an echo in her ears, like voices rising from a deep, dark well. "Ribbit . . . ribbit . . . ribbit!"

She bolted up and looked around frantically, expecting to find herself back in the bedroom of her parents' castle with either a prince on her floor or a frog on her pillow.

She was relieved to find neither.

Instead of her parents' castle, she was in her small dorm room at school, in a place most people called "the real world," about as far from Once Upon a Time as she could get. She was not a lonely, rebellious princess—not anymore—but one student among many at the Home Educational Academy.

The Home Educational Academy—or HEA for short—was not like other boarding schools, though it tried to be. It was the cornerstone of the Princess Protection Program.

The school offered classes in all the usual school

subjects, like math and reading and history and science, but the students of HEA had a unique set of needs that the school also tried to meet. There were classes in sword fighting, curse breaking, and riddle solving. There were also classes in fashion, technology, and even a class called Introduction to Snack Food, which was as mysterious to the students as a witch's riddle. In fact, most of the students at HEA had more experience with witch's riddles than with modern snack food.

Rana sighed with happy relief as she looked up at the moon through her window. She'd dozed off at her desk, drooling on her biology textbook, right on the page about dissecting frogs. She'd been studying since dinnertime. *That* must have caused her nightmare.

She stood and stretched and ran her finger along the colorful Mohawks and Motocross PunkFest poster that hung crooked on the wall above her desk, just as she'd meant it to. Anyone could hang a poster straight, but what could be more punk rock than hanging it crooked on purpose?

She smiled. She was home. There were no frogs stalking her here. The voices of her friends in the common room carried down the hall. She rose to join them.

Six princesses and one prince were in the middle of an important conversation. They lounged on a hard gray sofa and two armchairs arranged around a low wooden coffee table.

In fairy tales, the furniture for princesses was intricately decorated and made from fine fabrics, and walls were covered in tapestries and oil paintings. In the real world, the common room was designed for practicality. The furniture was durable and stain resistant and came from a mysterious store called Ikea. The walls were decorated with posters that just showed different shapes and colors and came from the same store as the furniture.

This strange decor was not, however, the topic with which the princesses (and one prince) were currently engaged. They had much bigger concerns.

"What *is* an Oreo and why are there so many different ways to eat one?" wondered Rosamund, studying the black-and-white sandwich cookie in her hand and the cold glass of milk in front of her. Rosamund was the newest student at the Academy, having fled her story after waking from a hundred-year sleep to an unwelcome kiss, and she still had a lot to learn.

"It's just a cookie," said Margaret, who was known as Snow White before she arrived at HEA.

The Academy was designed and built for fairy-tale princesses (and two princes, and three unicorns disguised as teenaged boys), all of whom were unhappy with how their tales went. Being the main character in a fairy tale was . . . well . . . no fairy tale.

Fairy tales—the real ones—were not cute bedtime stories with happy endings for all involved. The real ones hid hungry ogres and wicked witches. They were filled to the brim with magic and bloodshed, tragedy and trickery, and too often for the princesses, weddings. So many weddings.

Boarding school was a better option. There were no weddings here, just homework, and no ogres, just Oreos.

"There are not *so many* different ways to eat an Oreo," Sirena explained. "There is *one* way: you dunk the cookie. Like this."

"I didn't know there were rules for this sort of thing," said Rosamund. "It's just a cookie."

"It's not *just* a cookie. It's the *best* cookie. And there *aren't* any rules for how to eat it," Rana announced as she threw herself down beside Rosamund and dangled a leg over the armrest of the sofa in a very un-princessy way. "There is no wrong way to eat an Oreo. Some people like to twist the halves apart and lick the cream off the sides or dunk the halves into the milk one at a time."

"Rana is correct," said Cindy, their Princess Orientation Peer and the unofficial leader of their dormitory. "You may eat the cookie however you please." The regal, dark-skinned princess cast a disapproving look at Sirena, then added one of her perfectly beatific smiles. "But I'm also a fan of dunking."

She snatched an Oreo from the open container and dunked it in the glass of milk, already speckled with cookie crumbs. She closed her eyes in bliss as she chewed.

"You know, you could just not dunk the Oreos at all," suggested Charlie, his mouth stuffed with two dry cookies at once, spitting crumbs everywhere. He should know better, but some things were impossible to teach a prince, like table manners.

"Now that Rana's here, can we start the dance committee meeting?" asked Sirena. "If we don't use our time well, our school's first ever dance will be a disaster!"

"I thought worrying about time was Cindy's thing?" said

Rana. "On account of her trouble with midnights."

"Everyone knows nothing good happens after midnight." Cindy sniffed. "But our dance ends well before that, so I'm not worried about a thing."

"Well, I *am*," Sirena told them. "I want this to be the best dance the school has ever had."

"It will be," Cindy assured her. "Because it's the *only* dance the school has ever had."

"I thought we came to this world to get away from all the fancy balls," Rana told them. She had zero good memories of the balls at her parents' castle. They were stuffy affairs, with boring music, where she wore uncomfortable dresses and was forbidden from talking to anyone or dancing with anyone except her father. And even then, every step of her dance had to be perfect.

"It's not a ball," Sirena reminded her. "It's a *school dance*, which is something that happens all the time in the real world, and it's not fancy, it's fun!"

"How can it be fun?" asked Bea. "There are like three hundred girls at this school, and only five boys. The ratio is off." Bea had been stuck in a castle with one beastly boy and very much preferred having more options in the real world.

"I don't think the ratio is off," said Margaret.

"You did live alone with seven mountain-mining dwarves," Rana reminder her. "I'm not sure we should trust your judgment on this."

"There *aren't* only five boys," Rosamund corrected Bea. "This isn't one of our stories. In the real world, we don't know everyone's gender. I don't think the Einhorn brothers are even boys at all, though that is their human disguise. They're unicorns, and unicorns don't live by the same rules humans do. They're two-thirds made of starlight."

"Now I think *your* ratio is off," said Charlie. "They're at least half cotton candy, energy drink, and deodorant."

"That's three halves," Cindy corrected him.

"Hey, they don't live by the same rules humans do!" Charlie repeated, grinning.

Rana laughed and gave Charlie a high five, both because she loved irking Cindy and because she loved anything that made rules look like nonsense, whether it was unicorn math or Oreos. In fairy tales, the rules were ironclad. In the real world, everything changed all the time and people who thought they knew exactly how things should be usually turned out to be totally wrong. If you weren't afraid to ask questions, you could upend any rule in existence. It was her favorite thing about the real world.

"I just think we need more boys, that's all," said Bea.

"A dance isn't about boys and girls; it's about dancing." Cindy brushed some cookie crumbs from her school blazer, a small gesture done with such grace that everyone else hung on her every word. If anyone knew about the point of dances, it was Cindy. "The students at this school could use more dancing in their lives."

"I agree!" said Sirena, clapping. Now that she had legs, she wanted to use them for everything that they could possibly do. She ran, she played basketball, she did yoga, and most of all, she danced. "We need to discuss decorations. Danny Einhorn volunteered to have his brothers make them, but those unicorns can get kinda—"

"Tacky?" suggested Rana.

"I was going to say *exuberant*," said Sirena, "but yes, unicorn style is an acquired taste. I suggest we pick a theme to keep them in check."

"What about Under the Sea?" suggested Margaret, and everyone sucked in their breath. Sirena froze, clenched her jaw, and then smiled again.

"I think not," she said calmly. "Other ideas?"

"Winter Wonderland!" suggested Elise, a former ice princess.

"A Magical Menagerie!" suggested Bea.

"Punk Rock!" shouted Rana. She'd meant to play it cooler, but unlike Elise, she had no chill. She cleared her throat, trying to act like she hadn't been thinking about it nonstop for weeks. "I mean . . . if it's a *dance*, we'll need music . . . I could even, you know . . . perform."

She smiled sheepishly. This was her first chance, ever, to play live music in front of people. Her music. She *loved* punk rock. It was loud; it was chaotic; it followed no rules! It was, in short, the opposite of her life in her story. Her parents would hate it, but it was everything she wanted to be. And she wanted to share the *real* her with everyone else. It was the only reason she'd volunteered to be on the dance committee in the first place.

"Oh Rana, I didn't know you wanted to play at the dance," said Sirena, which Rana noticed was not an invitation to do so.

"Well, I do," she told her friends.

"But . . . I mean . . . you . . . er . . ." Bea blushed.

"It's just that . . ." Sirena trailed off and avoided looking at her.

Rosamund leaned forward and rested a hand on Rana. "Honey, punk rock is kinda angry for a school dance."

The others stared at Rana with pitying eyes, which was almost worse than if they'd simply told her no, or laughed at her, or turned her into a frog.

"I love you, Rana," Sirena told her. "But your music is like a beached whale six weeks after a summer hurricane."

"That's a very specific image," noted Rana.

"Well, I *was* a mermaid," said Sirena. "And I know music. Also whales."

"She means it's rotten," Margaret explained.

"I think it sounds a bit more like wolves howling," said Bea. "That's not *all* bad."

"More like wind through a frozen cavern," said Elise. "Not something that makes you want to dance."

"I got it," Rana grumbled. "But if you'd give it a chance, you'd see punk can be whatever you want it to be. It's not *just* angry music. It's fun and disobedient and—"

"Loud," said Cindy. "And not very pretty."

"Well, of course it's not pretty!" Rana found herself

standing, throwing her arms in the air. The others flinched. They thought she was just defending her taste in music, but she was defending herself, her very *being*.

Punk is who I am! she wanted to shout. *If you dislike punk, you dislike me!*

Instead, she said, "It has to be loud to shake the foundations of the world! And haven't you had enough of pretty? I don't want to be pretty! I want to make walls crumble and kingdoms fall."

"You're describing a siege, not a song," said Cindy. "Maybe you should consider military school?"

Rana looked at the concerned faces of her friends around the common room. Her heart was thundering like a double bass drum. Maybe she'd gotten too upset. They didn't know what this music meant to her, at least, not yet. But she'd get them to understand.

"Look. Don't answer now," she urged. "I promise, by the time of the dance, you'll *want* me to play my music. Trust me." She smiled. "Now, enjoy the rest of your cookies . . . in whatever ways you choose to eat them."

She curtsied curtly to the group and left them to finish their dance discussion and Introduction to Snack Food homework, while she rushed across campus.

She had an appointment for private guitar lessons with one of her teachers, lessons she needed now more than ever, and she did not want to be late.

She usually was late.

She couldn't exactly explain that she'd been accidentally napping and then arguing with the dance-planning committee. That wasn't a very punk rock reason to be late that her teacher would understand.

However, when Rana climbed the stairs to the second-floor music room, instead of Professor Perrault in his too-tight orange sweater with his old guitar and book of musical scales, she found a huge dragon waiting for her, orange scales gleaming. The beast had hunched between the whiteboard and the piano, and its snout sizzled with flame.

Rana could not contain her smile.

CHAPTER TWO
Not with a Roar, but with a Ribbit

Rana's teacher was not like most teachers. In fact, the fiery dragon *was* her teacher. Though Professor Perrault normally did not change into his true dragon form, everyone knew he was one and could transform anytime he felt like it.

When she walked in on him spitting fire in the classroom, he had a beautiful black electric guitar in the shape of a lightning bolt strapped around his neck. It looked tiny in his giant dragon claws, but it was plugged in, and one of his giant dragon feet was resting over a hot-pink pedal connected to an amplifier. The volume on the speaker was cranked up all the way past ten.

Professor Perrault nodded toward a beautiful golden electric guitar in a stand opposite, plugged in and begging to be played.

Rana rushed to it. She'd been waiting for this lesson for

months. This was the greatest sign of respect a dragon guitar teacher could show. Rana was about to jam with a real dragon!

Professor Perrault couldn't talk when he was transformed, so he just grunted for her to hurry up. She slung the strap over her shoulder, snatched up the pick, got her hands in position, and readied herself to rock.

The dragon tapped one huge orange foot to mark the beat, and Rana counted aloud.

"A one and a two and a one-two-three-four!"

Then she and the dragon roared together, not with their mouths, but with their axes, which was, Rana thought, the best nickname for a guitar, because an axe was something out of a fairy tale, something that slayed monsters.

Rana stretched her fingers across the frets on the neck of her axe, forming one power chord after another. She strummed her other hand up and down over the strings, screeching out music that was meant to sound like dragons battling in the sky over an active volcano.

She closed her eyes and tried to find the beat. Tried to keep her fingers at the pace of her teacher's claws. She imagined herself in a huge stadium, standing in the center of the stage, thrashing out on the guitar as 63,280 people cheered and sang along to her song. She leaped through the air; she howled and hooted and spun; she kicked over a stand of lights and windmilled her guitar around over her head. She was wild, feral, out of control . . . and the crowd loved it.

They loved *her*.

They roared their approval. They spat out her lyrics like fire, so hot it singed her hair all the way on the arena stage.

Her eyes snapped open. She was not in an arena. There was no crowd, nor giant stands of lights. She'd kicked over a rolling whiteboard. She'd knocked everything off the teacher's desk. She'd gotten lost in her fantasy and only the teacher spitting actual fire had stopped her. The room reeked of burnt hair.

"Sorry," she said. "I guess I got carried away."

As she watched, her teacher shrank down into his human size again, his wings folding in and becoming his too-tight orange sweater, his scales forming pants, and his face glowering with just the same angry expression he'd worn as a dragon. Except now, instead of roaring and spitting fire, he could talk, and he sounded disappointed.

"Rana, Rana, Rana," he sighed, setting his guitar back in

its stand. "You could be so great if you would slow down and pay attention to the basics. Finger placement, scales, and chord progressions. You let your passions run away with you."

"But punk music is all about passion," she said.

"*Music* demands precision," her teacher replied. "Only when you've mastered the rules can you begin to break them."

"But punk isn't about *rules*! That's the whole point!" she whined, and realized that punk was *also* not about whining. "Sorry." She set the guitar down and started to clean up everything she'd knocked over. She did not want to act like a brat. That's not who she was anymore. "I just *feel* the music so powerfully."

"The challenge," her teacher told her, "is to make your fingers match your feelings. And that takes practice. As my mother used to say, you have to sizzle before you can scorch."

"Then that's exactly what I'll do," promised Rana. She had to prove to the others that her music could be perfect for the dance.

For the next hour, she ran scales and scales and more scales. Dragons, true to form, loved scales. The professor tapped his foot to keep time and when she fell off the beat, he shouted so loud it made her miss his dragon roar.

Rather than complain, though, she clenched her jaw and got back to work. This was what it took.

She practiced long after the professor left, long after a less motivated princess would've stopped. That was the difference between hard work in a fairy tale and hard work in the real world. This was work she chose to do. She strummed and picked and stretched her hands past anything they'd ever done before. She'd be tired the next morning, but she didn't care. She just wanted to rock.

It was late when she finally stopped playing and set her shiny golden guitar back in its stand. Her arms shook. Her finger ached. She had to get a cloth to wipe smears of blood from the strings. *That*, she thought, *is very punk*.

By the time she'd started across campus toward bed, the moon hung fat and full at the top of the sky.

It was near midnight, which some called the witching hour. As her friend Cindy knew well, midnight was an important time in fairy tales, when magic worked or stopped working, when curses were lifted or curses fell, when fates were sealed and doors were opened.

In the real world, midnight was just really, really late.

Exhausted, she trudged along the path that led back to the dorms and reached the place where it skirted the outer fence of the Academy. She thought she heard a familiar sound, which stopped her in her tracks. It was hard to tell because her ears still rang from practice, and she cocked her head to listen.

"Ribbit. Ribbit."

She looked around.

"Ribbit. Ribbit."

Rana shuddered. There were no frogs at the Academy and if there had been she would have long ago tossed them out. She wanted no reminders of her past, of the demanding frog prince who'd followed her home or the castle where she'd been forced to entertain him.

"Hello?" she called into the darkness and didn't like the way her voice quivered. She cleared her throat and called again with confidence. "Whoever's there better show themselves. I am not someone you want to mess with. I know jujitsu and krav maga and fencing and karate and ballet."

The last one might not have sounded so intimidating to anyone who had never met a ballerina, but for those who knew, ballerinas were strong and tough and had no fear of pain. Rana wouldn't want to mess with one. "Show yourself before I drag you into the moonlight!"

"Ribbit," said a frog just on the other side of the fence, off school grounds. She wrinkled her nose.

"Ugh, disgusting," she said.

She'd always thought frogs looked like a heap of boogers sculpted by an ill-mannered toddler, and this one was a perfect example of what she meant. Its eyes were bulging and twitching and looking in opposite directions. Its face was somehow pointy and blunt at the same time, and its greenish skin was covered in lumps and bumps like warts on a witch's nose. It snapped out its tongue and ate a passing gnat.

"Gross," she told it. "Get out of here."

The frog stared back at her from the other side of the fence and she saw something like sadness in its big, blinking eyes.

"Look, sorry," she said. "It's just . . . I have bad history with a frog. Could you please leave?"

"Ribbit," repeated the frog.

"Whatever," she told it. "It's late, and I'm tired, and

you're only some stupid frog."

She was about to leave when the frog flexed its little legs and hopped right through the space between the fence posts. It landed with a wet plop in front of Rana's feet. "Ah!" She startled and fell backward, landing on her bottom with a hard *thwap*.

"Apologies for startling you," said a voice as soft as new velvet, and Rana stared up from the dirt at a dashingly handsome prince, his strong hand extended to help her to her feet.

For a fleeting moment, she almost looked for the frog, but then her mind caught up, and she understood the situation perfectly.

"Oh," she grunted. "It's you."

CHAPTER THREE
A Hopped-Up Prince

Rana stood without the prince's help and wiped the dirt from her guitar-blistered fingers on her school skirt. It was the prince's turn to frown. But instead, he smiled.

"It's wonderful to see you again, Princess Rana!" He bent at the knee and reached again for her hand, probably to kiss it. She folded her hands together behind her back.

"I'm just Rana here," she said. "We don't have royal titles."

"Ah, but you are my princess, wherever I find you," he declared, his eyes shining green in the moonlight. "Were I to find you in a cave or a trash heap or in the belly of a beast, I would still see only your perfection."

"Why would I be in a trash heap?" she demanded. "Do you think I'm trash?"

"Er, um . . . er . . ." The prince's face flushed. "What I meant was, *if* you were in a trash heap . . . not that you *would* be . . . you're . . . um . . ." The prince recovered himself and stood up tall, resting a hand upon his heart to strike a princely pose. He cleared his throat and began a speech that he'd obviously rehearsed. "Ever since you ran from the castle, I have searched for you. I have crossed worlds to find you on nothing but frog legs and hope, the hope of seeing your beauteous visage once more and laying a promised kiss upon your perfect cheek."

She was unimpressed. Speechifying was, like, the main thing princes did. She'd have been more impressed if he hadn't given one.

"I never promised you a kiss." She looked him up and down in a way she hoped came across as withering. "You made that part up."

"All our stories are made up," he said. "I simply choose to make mine up with you."

Rana rolled her eyes. The prince wore a pale pink shirt and a green velvet waistcoat with green velvet pants, tied with a sash. The same outfit he had been wearing after she'd tossed him against the wall in her bedroom. His brown hair swooped handsomely over his brow, and even the silver toe caps on his black boots shone. He looked terribly out of place in the real world.

"You should *not* be here," she said, glancing around to make sure no one was watching them. She did *not* want anyone to see her chatting up a frog prince with no respect for personal boundaries. "You should leave. Right now."

"Will you come with me?" he asked. "My curse is not yet lifted, not until I unite with the one who truly loves me."

"I'm not going with you," she told him. "I don't love you, and *stalking* me is no way to make me fall in love with you."

"I am not stalking you!" he cried out. "I helped you find your golden ball and in exchange you agreed to—"

"I remember what I agreed to!" she said, cutting him off.

"Well, an agreement is a sacred bond," said the prince. "You have to understand, princess, the rules must be followed."

"Are you frog-splaining fairy tales to me?" she asked.

Rana thought she'd left her story and its rules and this frog behind. Wasn't the whole point of the Princess Protection Program that no one from her tale should be able to follow her? Especially here, in the place she felt safest in the world?

She remembered her promises, of course. How could she

forget what she'd said to the gross little frog by a well in the woods, or the command her parents gave that she fulfill the frog's gross little wishes?

"You made a promise and then you ran away," the prince said.

"I *kept* my end of the bargain."

"Not until I followed you. And then you threw me into a wall and disappeared!"

"I threw you into the wall of *my room*," she clarified. "Our deal was that you be allowed in my room, and so you were. I never agreed to stay with you and certainly not to fall in love and marry you!"

"But that's how the story goes," he whined. "It's called 'The Frog Prince.' That's me. And you are my princess!"

"Not anymore."

The prince looked around, taking in his surroundings. "Where are we anyway? Are you a prisoner here? Is there some witch I must battle or dragon I must defeat?"

"Absolutely not!" Rana cried. "This is a school! Our headmistress sometimes sounds like a witch, but she's an actual fairy godmother. Madame Phoebe looks out for us. And the dragon is teaching me how to play guitar."

The prince kicked his toe into the dirt and blinked in a very frog-like way. "The thing is . . . I *need* you to come back."

"Not a chance." She crossed her arms and planted her feet, making it clear that she was not the least bit tempted.

"It's not fair," he said. "I'm trapped as a frog *until* you come back."

"Well, I didn't turn you into a frog. Why should I have to turn you back?"

"Your name is Rana! It literally means frog in Latin!" He threw his arms in the air. "We're tied to one another by destiny. You have to!"

"I don't believe in destiny," said Rana. "And I don't believe in princes telling me what I have to do."

"Do you believe in helping people?" he asked.

"Of course," she told him. "And unlike *you*, I don't demand anything in return."

"Then *help* me," he pleaded, dropping to one knee. "If you don't come back with me, I will turn into a frog again."

"Why aren't you a frog right now?"

"Because curses don't work inside the school fence," said

Cindy, stepping from the shadows. "Ever since Madame Phoebe became headmistress. She cast a spell that blocks curses on campus."

"How long have you been listening?" Rana asked.

"Long enough to hear how you made a promise to this frog prince," said Cindy.

"You see, I told you—" the frog prince began, but Cindy cut him off by holding up a single finger.

"*And*," she added, "to hear how you kept your end of the bargain before leaving your story. As far as I can tell, that makes you two even."

"Ha!" said Rana.

"She threw me at a wall!" the frog prince whined.

"You were not respecting her boundaries," said Cindy.

The prince clasped his hands to beg. "Please return to my story with me! Nothing can happen until you return. Everyone is just kind of . . . waiting. Your parents, your friends."

"I didn't have any friends," said Rana sadly. She could feel Cindy giving her a pitying look, although as far as Rana knew, Cinderella didn't have any friends in her story either. Though she did have a fairy godmother at least. Rana wasn't as lucky as that.

"Well, *my* friends miss me," said the prince. "Terribly. And *I* miss *you*."

"You didn't even know me," Rana told him. "And I didn't know you. I don't even know your name."

"I am Prince Sebastian," he said. "Now you know me."

"Hardly." Rana huffed.

"I won't leave without you," he said, crossing his arms just like she had crossed hers. Not to be imitated, Rana uncrossed her arms. Prince Sebastian uncrossed his.

"Stop it!" she yelled at him. "Stop copying me! Stop following me! Stop trying to manipulate me!"

Her temper got the better of her, and she stormed off, leaving Cindy and Prince Sebastian alone together in the moonlight. As she walked away, she could feel shame bubbling up inside her belly like she'd put too much hot sauce on a Tater Tot. She'd acted like just the sort of brat she'd been in her story, and she didn't want to be that person anymore. That was who she *used* to be, not who she was now, in the real world. She stopped herself, took a deep breath, and turned back around.

And smacked right into the prince again.

"Did you listen to anything I said?" she blurted.

"Sorry!" said Cindy from beside him. "We aren't following you. I'm just taking him to see Madame Phoebe."

"But . . . why?"

"I asked to become a student here," Prince Sebastian said proudly. "Cindy told me what this place is for, and since I am unhappy with my story, I'd like to enroll."

"What?" Rana was incredulous, incensed, irritated, and every other irate *I* word she could think of. "I . . . I . . ." She'd also become inarticulate.

"I have as much right to be here as you do," Prince Sebastian said to her. "If you won't come back with me, then I shall stay here with you . . . and stay human too."

"But you can't!" Rana objected and looked to Cindy. "He can't!"

"Why not?" the prince asked.

"Why not?" Cindy asked.

"Because . . . he's the reason I left my story and came here in the first place!"

Cindy shook her head. "I know you better than that. You didn't leave because of some creepy frog prince in your bedroom."

"I'm not creepy . . . ," Sebastian mumbled, but the girls ignored him.

"You left because you were stifled by the rules of your kingdom. He was just the last straw."

"Well, maybe," Rana agreed.

"And it'd be wrong to turn him away," Cindy said. "We help those in need. Even if they've been wretched little toads to us in the past."

"I was not wretched," Prince Sebastian mumbled, but again found himself ignored.

"Fine," Rana grunted. "But I want nothing to do with him." She jabbed a finger at his chest. "I have a lot to do before our first-ever school dance, and *you* will not get in my way. Not to demand my attention, affection, or so much as a smile from me, got it?"

"But your smile is so beautif—"

The look Rana and Cindy gave him could've boiled a frog.

He held his hands up in surrender.

"I am *not* responsible for you," Rana said, and found it felt good to speak her mind instead of running away. "I didn't make you into a frog, and I'm not the one to unmake you, got it?"

He nodded, wide-eyed.

With that, Rana stormed off to her room and let Cindy lead the frog prince to wake Madame Phoebe, the headmistress. As their paths parted, she heard Prince Sebastian tell Cindy, "I love how *assertive* she is."

Rana rolled her eyes but couldn't help smiling. She loved that about herself too. *Speaking my mind to some prince who thought he was the end of my story? Ha! What could be more punk rock than that?*

But she tossed and turned all night in her bed, dreaming that a hundred frogs were chasing her through the deep, dark woods.

CHAPTER FOUR

The Student and the Frog

Madame Phoebe enrolled Sebastian and gave him a uniform that very night. In the days that followed, Rana did her best to avoid him.

If Sebastian sat in the back in math class, she sat in the front. If he ran the mile in gym class in nine minutes, she ran it in eight minutes. When he fainted during the frog dissection unit in biology class, she jumped right into the assignment, scalpel ready. Even their teacher shuddered at her eagerness.

"I get it," Rosamund told her as they shuffled between classes. "If the prince from my story showed up here, I'd be annoyed too."

"I'm not *annoyed*," Rana told her, annoyed. "I'm not thinking about him at all. He might as well still be a frog."

This was clearly untrue. She couldn't *stop* thinking about him, and he was definitely not still a frog. He was very much a prince and he was always wherever she was, lurking, waiting for her to pay attention to him, just like he'd been waiting at that well when she'd dropped her golden ball.

He can wait forever, she thought. *I am never going back with him to that fairy tale.*

"Princess, if I could just talk to you." He chased after her between classes. "I'm really a nice guy! All my friends say so! My best friend, Heinrich, he tells me how great I am all the time!"

"Heinrich? You mean your *servant*?" Rana scoffed. "Doesn't he *have* to tell you how great you are? It's his job."

"When I got turned into a frog, he never abandoned me," said Sebastian. "And that was totally not his job. He did it for friendship!"

"Why are you telling me this?"

"Because I need you to fall in love with me!"

"You can't argue someone into falling in love with you, just like you can't bargain for it," Rana told him. "You can't force it."

"Then I can wait for it!" Sebastian smiled. "I will wait for you until the end of the world, my dear Rana. You're my destiny."

"Ugh," Rana groaned. She just wanted to be left alone to practice guitar. "I think I liked you better as a frog."

When they split into groups for a new project in Introduction to Snack Food, Sebastian tried to be in her group, so she switched to Margaret's, even though their assigned snack was rice cakes, and Sebastian's group got Cool Ranch Tortilla Balls.

"Each group will present an argument for why their snack is superior, and the class will vote on the winner at the end," said Professor Calonita.

Rana made the best case she could for the health benefits of a snack that tasted like cardboard and felt like Styrofoam, but of course her team lost when Sebastian, Bea, and Charlie argued that no health benefits could outweigh the cheesetastic goodness of cool ranch flavoring.

"I learned a new word today." Sebastian grinned at her after class, turning on all his charm. "Cheesetastic."

"That's not a word," said Rana. "Charlie just made it up."

"All words are made up," said the prince. "But I like this one. It describes what it means perfectly. An ecstasy of cheese! An exuberance of cheddar! A taste explosion of most epic propor—"

"Could you please not give a romantic speech about Cool Ranch Tortilla Balls?" Rana interrupted him.

"I'd rather give a romantic speech about my love for you," he said. "But you've made it quite clear you don't want me to do that."

Rana's eyes were getting tired from rolling them at Sebastian all the time. In fairy tales, a prince devoted to the pursuit of a princess was supposed to be romantic, but in reality, it was truly tiresome.

When the Einhorn brothers invited Sebastian to play no-teams basketball, Rana was relieved to get a break from him at the dance-planning committee. At least there, things were normal.

"We should have cupcakes," suggested Margaret. "Everyone loves cupcakes."

They all agreed, and Cindy wrote it down.

"We should have pizza," suggested Sirena. "Everyone loves pizza."

They all agreed, and Cindy wrote it down.

"We should have live music," suggested Rana.

They all agreed, but Cindy did not write it down. They stared at her instead.

"Yes, I'm still suggesting I play," she admitted. "But, like, I can *prove* to you how good punk music is. I've been practicing!"

"We know," said Cindy. "The whole campus can hear when you practice."

"I told you, punk is supposed to be loud." Rana defended her music.

"But we want *pop* music," said Sirena. "Something people can dance to."

"You can dance to punk!"

"Slam dancing isn't really dancing, though," said Bea. "It's more like a bunch of boars fighting."

"This is the first dance," Sirena added. "I want it to be perfect."

"And my music would ruin it?" Rana's temper flared. She found tears welling in her eyes. Her friends couldn't see how much this meant to her. With the frog prince here at school reminding her of her past, and her friends wrinkling their noses at what she dreamed would be her future, the well of her feelings was dark and deep. She was about to cry in front of everyone, which was not very punk rock at all.

They still thought this was just about the music. But it

was about so much more! It was about rebellion! It was about freedom! It was about leaving behind the lonely princess she'd once been!

"What about *one* song?" she pleaded. "Can I play just one song?"

The girls looked at one another, all of them talking with their eyes. Suddenly, Rana was scared they were going to say no, and she couldn't bear the thought of this rejection.

Before they could answer, before anything bad could happen, she stood up. She hadn't decided to stand, or to ball her fists, or to make the pouty face she knew she was making. Anger and fear were like puppeteers, her worst emotions pulling her strings. She felt like a child throwing a tantrum. Worse, she felt like a *spoiled* child, throwing a tantrum because she hadn't gotten what she wanted. What next? Was she going to throw someone at a wall? Her head spun.

I'm not like that anymore! I wasn't ever like that here at a school, not until Prince Sebastian showed up! This is all his fault! Rana ran away before she could do anything worse.

"Rana!" Rosamund called as she stormed out of the room. "Wait! We're just going to—"

But Rana was already stomping down the stairs, two at a time, and bolting across campus to speak some more of her mind to that selfish frog prince whom she had definitely *not* invited to be a part of her new life in this world. She had new music, new friends, new dreams, and she'd be far better off if he just went away!

Her feet carried her to the basketball court, where she stood arms akimbo and glared at Sebastian. He made one jump shot after another, until Van Einhorn figured out that jumping was his only move, and blocked his next three attempts.

She waited for him to notice her and to step away from the game, sweaty and breathless, so she could confront him.

"Listen, frog boy," she said while he used his T-shirt to mop the sweat from his face. "It's time for you to leave. You're ruining my life!"

"How am *I* ruining *your* life?" Sebastian asked. "I'm just going to school and playing with my new friends."

"They're *my* friends!" Rana yelled, sounding way brattier than she wanted to.

"I think you're mad about something else and blaming it on me," Sebastian said. "I don't want to be a frog, so if you won't come back to the story, I have to stay here. You don't even care that I'll become a frog if I go back alone! You'd leave me like that forever, wouldn't you?"

"That's—!" Rana started to object, but what could she say? He was right. It was annoying how right he was.

She wasn't mad at him. She was mad that her friends didn't love her music, and she was mad that the prince reminded her of the past, and she was mad that being mad had made her cruel. She didn't want to be a cruel person.

On the court behind them, RB Einhorn had briefly turned himself into a unicorn to kick the basketball with his hind legs.

"Hey, it's no teams, not no rules!" objected his brother Van, turning himself into a unicorn to impale the ball on his horn.

"I should get back to them," said Sebastian. "The game kind of falls apart without me."

Rana's anger left her like hot cheese sliding off soggy pizza crust. She took a breath and relaxed her shoulders.

"I'm sorry," she said.

He perked up. "For leaving me?"

"I'm sorry for being mean to you since you got here," she

clarified. "I am *not* sorry for leaving. I am not sorry that I didn't marry you in our fairy tale. If you're going to stay, you have to accept that. My future is here in this world, not back in yours. But I won't make you go back either. That wouldn't be fair."

The prince chewed his lip, considering. "So I guess you don't want to go to the dance with me?"

"Pah!" She laughed in his face. "Don't push it, bub! I'd rather dance with an enchanted pumpkin." She smiled at him, though, and even squeezed his shoulder affectionately. She could at least offer him that kindness after how she'd acted.

"Hey! Dude!" Danny Einhorn yelled over from the basketball court. "You coming back or what? No-teams basketball isn't as much fun with just my brothers!"

"Yeah!" the other two Einhorns agreed. "We need a human with us or else it's just *horsing around*!"

The three unicorns fell over each other laughing.

"Are they always like this?" Sebastian asked her.

"Yep," said Rana. "Unicorns have the *worst* sense of humor, but you'll grow to like it."

"This place is pretty magical," he told her, watching the

three brothers try to make themselves cough up rainbows by punching each other in the stomach. "It's weird too," Sebastian added. "But I see why you like it."

"And you haven't even tried pizza yet!" Rana told him with a grin.

"Rana!" Rosamund came running across campus with the other princesses just behind her. "There you are! You left before we could tell you! We talked about it, and of course you can play at the dance! We shouldn't have been so quick to brush you off."

Rana beamed. "Really? I can play the dance?"

"You can play *at* the dance," Sirena clarified. "Two songs. Not the whole dance."

"Two? I'll take it!" Rana clapped. A warm feeling flooded her. She'd made her peace with the frog prince and her friends had found a compromise that would make them all happy. It turned out, betting on a little kindness was always a winning move. That wasn't very punk, but it wasn't punk in the best possible way.

"I think I'll dedicate my first song to you," she told Sebastian.

"You will?" He blushed, and all Rana's friends raised

their eyebrows in surprise.

"Yeah, it's called 'Go Eat a Fly'!"

"I've eaten enough of those for a lifetime." Sebastian laughed and everyone joined him.

Rana couldn't wait to tear the roof off the dance with her music. She was so happy about it that she hardly noticed the sound of croaking frogs from just outside the fence. Not one, but dozens, like a whole colony of the amphibian pests had gathered just beyond the Academy's gate.

It's probably just in my imagination, she thought. *I've been dreaming about frogs for days.*

She'd soon find out it was not her imagination at all.

CHAPTER FIVE

The Punk-Rock Princess

The theme of the school dance was Cloud Kingdom, and Madame Phoebe had given the Einhorn brothers permission to use a little unicorn magic to fill the gym with actual clouds and rainbows and wildflowers. The rest of the decorations came from a Party Superstore by the highway, where Margaret and Sirena went shopping with one of the teachers.

Rana stood alone by the candy table in front of the bleachers drinking a Dr Pepper, which was spicy and sweet at the same time. It tickled her tongue. The students had dressed in all sorts of interpretations of the school dance outfits they'd seen in movies, from puffy-sleeved dresses that had been out of fashion in this world for so long that they were coming back into fashion, to tuxedo T-shirts. Charlie wore a flower print tuxedo he'd made himself, while Cindy wore a full gown that would've been right at home back in her fairy tale.

"Yeah, those two do not belong together," Sirena noted.

Rana, partly in protest, partly in her own interpretation of an outfit she'd seen in a movie, wore a punk-rock getup of black jeans torn at the knees and a shredded T-shirt from a children's cartoon that she'd held together with safety pins. She looked punk, but didn't feel it.

She felt nervous about her first-ever performance. The butterflies in her stomach were slam dancing. She felt like she had to pee, although she'd already peed four times in the last hour. She kept tapping her heels on the ground.

"Your legs are bouncing like a sewing machine needle," said Rosamund.

"I just want to do a good job," said Rana.

She loaded her pockets with her favorite candy, gummy bears and sour worms, and something called Mentos, which she'd never had before, but liked the tube shape of their container.

"Careful with those," Professor Gidwitz warned her. "Mentos and soda are an explosive combination."

She looked around the decorated gym at all the princesses having so much fun dancing to the playlist Sirena had made. Who was Rana to interrupt their fun with her music? What if they hated it? What if she messed up? What if she was terrible?

"Feeling ready?" Cindy slid away from the dance floor to ask. "It's almost time for you to play! Why do you look green?"

Sebastian, who'd been standing nearby acting like he was studying the candy table, suddenly spun Rana around. "Is she turning into a frog? I thought there were no curses here!"

In a panic, he ran his hands over his own head, his face, his body, checking for signs of frog transformation.

"Relax!" Rosamund told him. "It's just an expression for being nervous."

"You know, Rana, if you throw up onstage, you can just act like you meant to," Cindy suggested sweetly. "No one will know it's not part of the show."

"You're not helping," said Rana.

"You ready to make some *noise*?" Van Einhorn called to the crowd from the stage. He let out a unicorn whinny, which is just like a horse's whinny, if the horse had swallowed a rainbow. Everyone cheered. "We've got a great treat for y'all tonight! Live, for the first time ever, the musical mayhem of Rana and the . . ." Van stopped. He shouted down to Rana. "What's your band called?"

"I don't have a band!" said Rana. "It's just me. Nobody else."

"No band?" Van shrugged. "Weird. Okay, well, get up here and make some noise for Rana and Nobody Else!"

"That's not a great band name," Sebastian told her. "You might want to rethink it."

She left him and made her way to the stage. Her axe waited in its stand. It was in tune and ready, and she brought up an instrumental track on the phone onstage, so she could play along and sing. *Technology has its uses*, she thought, *but this would be better with a live band behind me.*

Looking out over the gym while she strapped the guitar on, she thought about who she could start a band with. Cindy would probably be a good drummer, keeping everyone on beat, and Sirena had an amazing voice. Rosamund could probably play bass. They could be the Rebel Princesses or something.

The princes might feel left out, but they could form their

own band if they wanted to. Maybe the school could have a Battle of the Bands. That was something real-world schools did, right? At least, they did in movies.

She grinned and looked out at the sea of faces waiting to hear her play. Her nerves were calmer on the stage than they had been down on the dance floor, like when you're standing on a rock, terrified to jump into a cool lake, but once you're falling, it feels great. She felt great. Everyone was rooting for her. If she were going to fail, this would be the safest place in the world to do it, in front of her friends. She got her fingers into position on the frets, raised her hand with the pick high in the air, and leaned into the microphone.

"Y'all ready to rock!" she yelled.

"*Yeah!*" everyone yelled back.

She noticed the teachers who'd been observing the dance shoving earplugs in and slipping out of the room. Madame Phoebe left too. Enduring live punk played by a former princess appeared beyond even her magical headmistress's abilities.

Their loss, Rana thought, and smiled.

"This is a song I wrote called 'Go Eat a Fly,'" she said into the microphone. She met her prince's gaze one more time, and he had such beaming admiration on his face that she hesitated. However misguided his feelings for her were, they were real, at least to him. She could respect that. "I'm dedicating it to my new friend Sebastian." The boy's face lit up. Charlie slapped him on the back fondly. "Who I hope will never have to eat a fly again!"

"Woo-hoo!" The audience cheered.

And then Rana's arm froze in the air.

She didn't shake the world with her song, or even belt out the first note. Her jaw dropped instead of her hand, and the amplifier hissed with ear-splitting feedback.

Murmurs spread. Everyone looked around, now seeing from the dance floor what Rana could see from the stage.

Standing right beside Sebastian was another prince, identical to him in every way except his outfit.

And on the other side of the room was another. And another. Three more entered through the door to the hallway, and four more came in the emergency exit. There were seven others scattered around in different outfits, and more kept showing up. Ten, then twenty, then thirty!

"Princess Rana!" one of them shouted up at her. "Come back with me! You gave your word, and I need your help!"

"No! With me!" another yelled.

"Come with me!" yelled still a third, and then they all burst out shouting at her to return with them to the fairy tale, and the sound they made shouting all together was like a frog pond at dawn, a cacophony of croaking and pleading.

"Who are all of you?" Sebastian cried out from the center of the dance floor, which made all the other frog princes pause and look at him and then at each other.

"I'm Prince Sebastian!" they all said in unison, and then fell to arguing with one another about which one of them actually was Prince Sebastian.

"What's happening?" Rana gasped as she stepped back from the microphone, heart beating louder than the song she wasn't getting to play. All these princes, too many princes, and all of them coming to drag her back to her tale? Was this a nightmare come alive?

She pinched herself to make sure she was awake.

She was.

A dozen new princes swarmed the dance now, all of them identical, all of them shouting for Rana's attention.

"You promised!" they yelled.

"I need you!" they yelled.

"Help!" they yelled, and their desperation sent a chill across Rana's skin.

Every one of them had a look of fear in his eyes. The only one who wasn't shouting at her was the one in his school uniform, the one she thought of as her prince, though in fact, she didn't know that for certain. What proof did she have that he really was from her story? That any of them were? She came from a world where witches could turn boys into frogs, so perhaps a witch could turn anyone into a boy? What if none of them were who they said they were?

But curses didn't work on school grounds, so every one of these Prince Sebastians must be in his real form, which was impossible. There could be only one, right?

They apparently thought so too, as they were all shoving and jostling to get her attention, claiming to be her prince. Her friends and classmates were as stunned as she was, watching the duplicates bicker, eyes wide and mouths agape.

Rana scanned the room for teachers before remembering they'd stepped out for her performance. There were no adults to help.

The frog princes must have noticed this as well, because that's when the first of them charged the stage to grab her.

"You must come back with me!" he cried. "Or we're doomed!"

CHAPTER SIX
A Whole Lot of Nothing

The prince shoved everyone out of his way as he leaped onstage and grabbed Rana's arm, hard. "Come with me, Princess! We must go back!"

"No, with me!" another yelled as he threw himself to the stage too. He hopped up in one frog-like leap and grabbed her other arm.

"Unhand her!" said a third prince, grabbing her by the shoulders. Only then did her original Prince Sebastian step up and command them all back.

"I don't know what sorcery this is, but she is mine, and you must all stand back, infernal cretins!"

"Who are you calling a cretin?" one of the duplicate princes said.

"Who are you calling 'yours'?" Rana said, yanking an arm free. She grabbed the Mentos from her pocket and her soda from the stool behind her. She remembered what

Professor Gidwitz had warned her about and dropped the candy into the soda.

The princes onstage looked at her with puzzlement.

Their puzzlement turned to shock as the soda bottle exploded with a geyser of foaming liquid. She aimed the jet of bubbling soda at the princes like a hose.

"Back!" she shouted. "All of you! Back!"

They fled the stage ahead of her candy chemical reaction.

In the chaos, her friends rushed to her side, taking up defensive positions around her.

"Someone better tell me what's happening!" she demanded. "You can't all be Prince Sebastian. There's only one real you!" She looked askance at the original in his school uniform.

"That, I am afraid, is not entirely correct," Madame Phoebe announced, strolling casually onto the stage in her purple silk robe, accessorized with flowing orange and pink scarves and bright, chunky jewelry. She looked every inch a fairy godmother turned magical headmistress, which was odd because she'd purchased her entire outfit at the Sunday craft market in the park behind the pizza shop in town. It just went to show that it was the person who made the magic, not the outfit. "They are all, as you can see, quite real."

"But there was only one Prince Sebastian in my story," Rana said.

"Not every story you're in is yours, dear," said Madame Phoebe, who didn't like to explain things more than she absolutely had to. Everyone waited for her to say more, which she did not.

"What does this mean?" Rosamund asked. "Is a sorcerer attacking the school?"

"Is it a spell gone wrong?" suggested Cindy.

"Or a curse gone right?" suggested Margaret.

"It's a broken story!" realized Rana. "Or . . . what do we call it?"

"A fractured fairy tale," said Cindy.

Madame Phoebe ran a hand along her smooth scarves and clicked her teeth. "Thankfully, Cindy pays attention to more than just snack food."

"Well, there are as many ways to eat an Oreo as there are ways to tell a story," explained Rosamund. "So they're kind of related."

Sirena added, "Every time someone tells a story like

'Cinderella in Space' or 'The Frog Prince' where the princess turns into a frog too"—Rana wrinkled her nose—"a new version is created."

"Now you're caught up. I never doubted you," said Madame Phoebe, whose tone made it clear that she had, in fact, doubted them. "There are more versions of all fairy tales than there are stars in the night sky," explained the headmistress. "An infinite number in fact. There are versions of 'The Frog Prince' that take place in the future, and under the sea, and in Delaware."

"What's Delaware?" asked Rana.

"No one knows," replied Madame Phoebe. "But each retelling creates its own reality, its own universe, running alongside ours. Parallel."

Rana scanned the crowd in front of her, all those identical faces. She'd never forget how that face looked the moment it had turned from frog to human against the wall of her bedroom in the castle, the moment she'd run away. She'd only dared look back once, and the prince calling out to her had looked so confused, so desperate.

Just like they all did now.

"So these princes are from different versions of my

story?" She shuddered. "And they *all* want me to go back? Don't their stories have their own . . . um . . . me's?"

"You vanished!" one of the princes called out.

"You were there one second and then, poof, gone!" another called.

"Something *took* you," said a third and the others concurred.

"Took me?" Rana's stomach clenched. The room felt colder. "Took me where?"

She looked to the doors of the gym, fearing she'd suddenly see fifty versions of herself burst in, all demanding to attend school here too.

The other princes didn't know, but one of them tried to explain what had happened to him. "I was lying against the wall of your room where you'd thrown me, looking up at you, when all of a sudden, this, like . . . shadow appeared. It grabbed you. The next thing I knew, you were gone."

"Same here!" called out another prince.

"That's about what happened to me too!"

A lot of them raised their thumbs and pinky fingers, shaking their hands in agreement.

"I went searching for you," another prince said. "I was a

frog again, so it took a while, but I wandered the woods and suddenly . . . I was at the gates of this school. And I felt like I just had to come in. When I did, I turned into me again. And then I followed the noise to find you here. My destiny."

"Same!" several of them shouted.

"You say it was a shadow that took her?" Madame Phoebe asked, peering down at the boys from the stage. She normally looked bored or put-upon when dealing with her students, but now she looked very serious, grave even.

Worse, thought Rana. *She looks worried.*

Rana had never seen the headmistress worried.

"What did this shadow look like?" Madame Phoebe asked the Prince Sebastian nearest her.

"Just a shadow," he said. "Darkness. Like something was blocking the light."

Madame Phoebe grunted at him. "Very helpful. Thank you for defining what a shadow is."

"You're welcome," he said.

"It was a shadow that blocked *all* the light," added another one. "It was the opposite of light. As though even shadows would fall into it."

"Did it have a shape?" Madame Phoebe pressed them,

and Rana looked at her friends, who were equally puzzled. "Like a person?"

"Hey, Mom?" Van Einhorn interrupted her from the back of the crowd in the gym. Madame Phoebe had taken in the unicorn triplets and created their human disguises, so they thought of her more as their mother than their fairy godmother or their headmistress.

"Not now, Van," she told him.

"Is this shadow thing dangerous?" Van asked her.

"If it is what I suspect, then, yes, it is very dangerous," she told him. "Now did the shadow look like—"

"Well, that's not great," Van interrupted her. "Because I think it's right here."

Every head in the room snapped around to look where Van was pointing, even Madame Phoebe's.

At first, Rana didn't know what Van was pointing at. All she saw were the cheap paper streamers strung among the bleachers, the puffy clouds floating in the rafters, and the rainbows between them, which were starting to fade and drip colorful puddles on the floor. The party lights cast shadows from the rafters this way and that.

But one shadow was different from the others. It was

darker than any shadow Rana had ever seen. It shed darkness the way the sun sheds light. It *glowed* dark.

And it moved.

It was shaped like a person but did not walk like a person. It glided across the floor like mist, and then its lightless arm reached out toward the nearest Prince Sebastian. He froze with fright, and the moment the shadowy hand touched him, his color faded to gray, to white, then to nothing.

He was gone.

The shadow cocked its featureless head, looking at the place where the prince had just been, as if it was confused. Then it turned toward another Prince Sebastian. Rana imagined that if the thing had eyes, it would have locked them on that one, who started to back away. The creature drifted toward him, the others scurrying out of its path. The prince it had targeted turned to run, but the shadow grabbed him and pulled him into a hug.

Just as before, the prince turned gray, then white, then disappeared, and the shadow stood hugging thin air. Again, it looked confused. Again, it swiveled its head around and locked an empty gaze on another Prince Sebastian. The thing didn't screech or roar or do a single monstrous thing, which made it all the more terrifying.

"Help!" the prince shouted.

Madame Phoebe sprang into action, producing a dry-erase marker from her sleeve and pointing it at the shadow. The marker began to glow. She swirled the magic wand once in the air and a circle of light appeared on the floor around the shadow.

"If light can contain you, I demand it explain you!" she chanted, and the thing turned toward her. It tried to reach out, but the light stopped it. Where it touched the circle of light, symbols appeared, written in shadows on the air. They vanished before Rana could make any sense of them, but Madame Phoebe nodded grimly.

"Well, this is unacceptable," she said.

"Were those runes?" asked Rosamund, who had read just about every book in the school library in her short time at the Academy.

"Yes," said Madame Phoebe.

"What did it say?" Rana asked.

"That it is an After," Madame Phoebe told them.

"As in happily ever after?" asked Charlie.

"Does it seem happy to you?" said Madame Phoebe. Charlie shook his head.

"What is it doing here?" Rana asked. "I thought no curses could get on campus?"

"It is not a curse," said Madame Phoebe.

"Some kind of evil magic?" asked Bea.

"Magic takes focus and self-control," said Madame Phoebe. "This has none. This is not magic. It is nothing, given form. And my magic does not work very well on nothing."

"What does it want?" asked Sebastian, on the edge of panic.

"It didn't say," said Madame Phoebe.

"So what happened to the princes it touched?" Rana asked. "Were they sent back to the stories they came from?"

"No," said the headmistress. "I fear that an After can only destory."

"You mean destroy?" Rana asked.

"No," said Madame Phoebe. "*De-story*. When an After touches something from a fairy tale, it is gone. Erased, removed from existence."

Rana looked at the shadow in the circle of light. It simply stood, unmoving, waiting.

"Can you stop it, Ma?" Danny Einhorn asked, his voice a worried whinny.

"This circle will only hold it a little while," she said. "It will escape, and it will continue to devour. A void, you see, wants only to be filled."

"How do we stop it?" asked Rana.

Madame Phoebe shook her head. "Why do you think I know?"

"You're a fairy godmother!" cried Rana. "How can you not know?"

"It's a strange and dangerous world we live in," said Madame Phoebe. "Sometimes not even a fairy godmother can tell you what to do."

"Look!" Cindy pointed at the circle of light. "It's fading. The After is going to get out."

Madame Phoebe shot another burst of light at it, rebuilding the circle, but it wasn't as bright as the first. She stumbled and the Einhorn brothers caught her.

"I'm afraid that's all the magic I can muster right now, children," she said weakly, and looked herself like a shadow had settled on her brow.

All the Sebastians started to panic, scrambling over one another to get away, climbing onto the stage, slipping on the sticky wet mess from the soda and Mentos explosion.

"What do we do?" asked Sirena.

"I think it's after me," said Rana. "The rest of you should run."

"We are *not* letting our friend face this alone," Rosamund declared. She stepped forward to stand by Rana and the Prince Sebastian she knew.

The others stepped up beside her.

"We're princesses from the greatest stories ever told," Cindy said, rallying all the students for battle. "We will not be defeated by some shadow that smells like gym socks."

"That's just, like, how the gym smells," said Charlie.

"It's gonna smell like victory!" Cindy raised a fist and the others cheered. Even the terrified Prince Sebastians cheered. It was hard not to feel inspired by Cindy's confidence. Rana looked around at her friends, at her headmistress, and at all these duplicate princes, and she felt ready to fight alongside them, but she also knew that none of them should *have* to fight at all.

This was not their fight.

The thing had shown up after all the Sebastians arrived, looking for her. She didn't know why, but she felt pretty sure she had caused this catastrophe.

This was *her* fight.

As the circle of light around the After flickered and faded, Rana jumped down from the stage. She turned her back to it, hoping she still had a moment before it was free. She wanted to face everyone for this.

"Listen to me!" she said. "You're all my friends and this school is my favorite place in the universe. It's the only place I've ever felt free to be myself. I'm grateful for that."

"Rana, what are you doing?" Rosamund started for her, but Rana held a hand up to keep her back.

"I can't let any of you be de-storied because of me," she said. "I couldn't live with myself if that happened."

"But we're ready to—" Cindy started.

"No!" Rana told her. "If this thing came here from my story, then I will defeat it!" She glanced back and saw the shadowy thing begin to slide past the last glimmers of Madame Phoebe's fading magic. She called to the Sebastians. "Follow me if you want to keep existing!"

With that, she ran for the door to the gym. The princes, every one of them, ran with her.

Just as she'd hoped, the shadow followed them and left her friends alone. It drifted after her, relentlessly but not quickly. She picked up the pace, and the Sebastians kept up with her.

"Do you have a plan?" her prince in his school uniform panted as he ran next to her.

"Not yet," she said. "Right now, I'm running."

"Back to our story?" he suggested hopefully.

"Not that either," she said.

Neither she nor her princes slowed until they reached the school driveway. They sprinted to the gate and straight through it. She wanted to put as much distance between her friends and the After as she could.

The moment they crossed out of school grounds, Rana found herself surrounded not by dozens of handsome princes, but by dozens of frogs, all of them hopping along beside her, bulging eyes darting, waiting for her to tell them what to do.

She had no idea.

CHAPTER SEVEN
Escaping Reality, Kind Of

Planning ahead was not Rana's strong suit, though running was, and she was fast. She hoped an idea would come to her as she ran, and the colony of frog princes hopped as fast they could behind her, desperate for a safety she wasn't sure she could find.

The shadow followed, but grew more distant with every stride. Rana felt good running; she felt heroic. With every footfall away from school, she was proving herself worthy of the faith her friends had shown in her. She was selfless and brave and . . . wet.

Several of the frogs had jumped onto her shoulders to hitch a ride and their slimy little feet tickled her neck and tangled in her hair.

"Yuck!" she yelled, and shook them off.

When they hit the pavement, she half expected them to turn into princes again.

They did not.

"I guess that only works in the story," she said.

"Guess so," said one of the frogs, sadly.

"So, what's the plan, princess?" asked another.

Rana glanced up the dark road. It was night and the moon cast shadows through the trees. The streetlights cast shadows too, and so did the lights from the town down in the valley. She didn't see the After, but it could be hiding in any one of those shadows.

She and the frogs had to keep moving, but they needed a destination. They couldn't just run all night. A shadow probably didn't need food and rest, but Rana and the frogs sure did.

She looked around at all of them. They were strangers, all except one of them. She searched among the frog faces, looking for anything to distinguish him from the rest. But they all looked about the same.

"Which one of you is my Sebastian?" she asked.

"I am!" they all croaked together.

"I don't know what you did to get cursed," she told them. "But it's really inconvenient right now."

"I was rude to a witch," one of them shouted.

"I was kind to a fairy," another confessed.

"I did nothing wrong!" said a third, followed by another croaking cacophony of excuses for what the frogs did or didn't do in their tales, and Rana had no way of knowing which was true, which was a lie, and most importantly, which was from *her* fairy tale.

"Okay . . . um . . . who can tell me one reason a rice cake is a superior snack?" she asked.

The frogs blinked at her. All but one. That one cleared his froggy throat and said confidently, "It is most certainly *not* superior to the Cool Ranch Tortilla Ball. No health benefits can outweigh the cheesetastic goodness of cool ranch flavoring." The frog puffed his throat proudly, and Rana scooped him from the pavement. She held the amphibious prince on her open palm just in front of her nose.

"We have a problem," she told him, then lowered her voice so the others couldn't hear. "I don't have a plan."

"Yes," he said at full volume. "You obviously do not have a plan."

"Duh!" the other frogs croaked out in chorus.

"Shhh!" Rana scolded them. "I'm speaking to the prince from *my* story, and I would appreciate it if you all could keep quiet."

"Isn't it more my story?" the frog prince asked. "I mean, it is called 'The Frog Prince,' not 'The Frog Princess.'"

"Well, maybe that was a mistake," she said. His webbed feet tickled Rana's hand. "What if you're the villain of the story?"

"What? How could I possibly be the villain?" Prince Sebastian was aghast.

"Think about it," said Rana. "You demand I offer my freedom in exchange for your help, then you stalk me—"

"I did not *stalk* you!"

"Then you *stalk me*," Rana pressed on. "To my house, to my dinner table, and to my bedroom. Even after I tell you no and flee, you follow me to this world. And you led the After here. Every action you take makes things worse. Hence: villain."

The frog raised one frog arm as if to object, but then stopped. He frowned, as much as a frog could frown, and his brow furrowed, as much as a frog brow could furrow. Rana wasn't sure frogs even had brows. Whatever it was that furrowed, however, the prince looked like he was thinking. All of the frog princes looked like they were thinking.

"I'm sorry," he said quietly.

"Excuse me?" Rana moved her hand closer to her ear.

"I said I'm sorry," the frog prince told her. "If I've acted villainously, I am sorry."

"*If?*"

"That!" he corrected. "I am sorry *that* I acted villainously. I shouldn't have forced you to take me in just to help you get your ball back. It was ungenerous of me. That's probably why the witch cursed me to begin with. I could be arrogant and self-centered."

Rana nodded. "Thank you," she said. "And I'm sorry for throwing you into a wall."

"Apology accepted," he said. "How about for leaving me?"

"I am not sorry for that," Rana told him. "Seems to me, the whole frog thing is between you and the witch who transformed you."

"That's not how our story works," he said. "You're the princess. Only you can turn me back. Just like with your friend Rosamund, who could only be awoken by a prince's kiss, or your friend Sirena, who could only stay human if the prince loved her. Or your friend Bea, who could only transform the beast into a human by loving him."

"Why do you think we're all *here* now?" Rana said, exasperated. "All the princesses at my school left their stories. But this is the first time an After has attacked. What's different about us? What does it want?"

The frog considered this. All the frogs considered it. They whispered to one another, and then Sebastian shrugged his little frog shoulders.

"I've no idea," he said.

"Me neither." Rana sighed. She needed an idea, and soon. She wasn't an expert in fairy tales or magic or curses or any of that stuff. She'd left it behind on purpose by escaping to the real world. But now, she needed someone who knew more about fairy tales than she ever could. She needed a scholar or a storyteller or a . . . well, she needed Rosamund, but she couldn't risk her friend being de-storied. Who else would have such voracious curiosity about fairy tales that they'd know—

The idea hit her like a bolt of lightning.

Neon lightning.

There, in front of her, was the neon sign for the Enchanted Woods Amusement Park, the fantasy theme park just up the road. The place where people were obsessed with fairy tales.

It was a risky idea, but it was the best one she had. She started moving again, glad to have a destination.

"Where are we going?"

"Into the woods," she told the prince.

He croaked once and looked anxiously among the moonlit birch trees, their bark as white as bones, their shadows deep and fearsome. Any one of those shadows could hold the After.

"Not those woods," Rana said, and pointed along the road. "*Those* woods."

Just ahead stood another gate, grander than their school's, but made of less sturdy stuff and far newer. The sign atop the gate was made to look like it was written in medieval handwriting, though it was in neon lights.

Both Madame Pheobe and the Academy's former headmistress had warned the students away from the Enchanted Woods and the people who worked there. Linger too long around pretend princesses and people would notice the difference. But in these circumstances, what better hiding place could there be?

"Where better to hide real fairy tales than among pretend ones? It's like hiding a scent from a bloodhound by surrounding it with other smells. This might be the safest place for you." She smiled at her own cleverness.

She led them to the gate of the amusement park, beyond which was a make-believe fairy-tale kingdom.

However, the ogre guarding the entrance blocked their path.

"Park's closing in fifteen minutes! No new entries!" he growled without even looking at her.

He was not an ogre, but rather a very hairy security guard, thick-bearded, heavy-lidded, with practically a pelt of hair almost as thick as his beard covering his arms. His massive body blocked the way in, and he even shifted himself to prevent her from peering around him. She caught a glimpse of people dressed just like her friends, costumed princesses and princes, and the tourists scrambling to meet them.

"Can I solve a riddle to get in?" she asked, because that's how it went in fairy tales.

The man bent down to look her in the eyes. His breath smelled like coffee and pickles. "A riddle? Sure!" He smiled with long yellow teeth. "What's short, and stout, and not getting into this amusement park?"

"Um . . ." Rana began to think.

"*You!*" The man guffawed. "Now you can stand out here all night or you can scram!"

Behind her on the road, a shadow drifted down the center of the lane, slowly but relentlessly. The guard didn't appear to notice, and it stopped outside the circle of lights on the edge of the parking lot.

It's uncertain if this light will trap it like Madame Phoebe's did, thought Rana.

Rana considered charging past the guard to get into the even more brightly lit amusement park, when suddenly, someone appeared on the other side of the gate to offer help.

"Oh there you are!" said a girl dressed exactly like Rana used to dress in her story. She looked like Rana too. She even had a frog perched on her shoulder.

Rana feared for an instant that her own fractured-fairy-tale selves were coming into this world, but then she noticed the frog was made of plastic and the girl's hair was a wig. The girl was simply costumed as her. And of course, they'd never met before, so it was very strange when the girl addressed the security guard. "Doug! You must let her in at once!"

"What?" said Doug, which did seem to Rana just the perfect name for the ogre of a man guarding the gate.

"Are you the reason she's late?" the costumed frog princess asked. "Because we have been *waiting*! She's the frog wrangler!"

"The frog wrangler?" Doug looked Rana up and down and looked at all her frogs sideways.

"You don't think I wrangle my *own* frogs?" The girl threw up her arms.

"Ribbit," said the frog prince. Rana grinned.

The girl continued to berate the guard, and he deflated like an old balloon. Doug waved Rana through with a grunt. She gave him a wink as she passed him, and all the frogs hopped into the amusement park behind her. The costumed girl took her arm.

"I'm not really the frog wrangler?" Rana whispered.

"I know," the girl whispered back. "My name's Skyler and I know *exactly* who you are. I know *what* you are too." She had a bounce in her step as she led Rana and her frogs into the park. "I'm honored to meet you. I have *so many* questions."

With that, the girl led Rana and her colony of frogs deep into the fairy-tale theme park, where lights blazed and music played and no shadows fell.

Rana glanced back to the gate and to the shadows beyond. She didn't know what this odd girl wanted from her and her frogs, and she wondered if she had miscalculated and traded one danger for another, after all.

CHAPTER EIGHT

The Boulevard of Make-Believe

The main street of the Enchanted Woods Amusement Park was called the Boulevard of Make-Believe. It was meant to look like a medieval village, with a grand fountain in the center and smaller streets leading away like spokes on a wheel. All the signs were hand-painted, and all the workers were costumed as medieval villagers, even if they were just taking tickets for rides or emptying trash cans or selling giant fried pickles on sticks that the guests could eat while they walked, dripping grease and vinegar onto their chins and their T-shirts and even—Rana noticed—their babies' heads.

The pretend village was packed, far more crowded than a real village would ever be. At least, Rana assumed so. She'd never actually been allowed to visit the villages in her parents' kingdom.

"Too dirty," her father had said.

"Too dangerous," her mother had said.

"And there is nothing interesting in the villages anyway!" added her father. "You'd find them quite boring."

There was nothing boring about this village though. Torches burned and flickered, lit as if by magic (though thanks to her classes, Rana knew they were likely on programmable timers and lit by electricity). The hand-painting on the signs burst into neon glow, revealing they weren't hand-painted at all. The neon lights didn't fit the theme, but looked very cool. To Rana's relief, they also kept the shadows away. Neither fairy-tale princesses nor fairy-tale amusement parks ever thought much about electricity bills.

The central fountain erupted into a show of dancing water and music and colorful lights, and several characters who looked like cheap imitations of Madame Phoebe rushed onto the streets, cheering and shooing people to stand by the side of the road.

"Are the workers here dressed like fairy godmothers?" Rana wondered.

"Of course," said Skyler. "Who better to keep things running and fix things when they break?"

Rana thought about Madame Phoebe, who didn't so

much fix things as give the princesses the tools to fix what was broken for themselves, usually with a snide comment. Fairy godmothers, when they were real, weren't often the solution to a princess's problems.

As they walked through the park, tourists snapped pictures, stopping to stare at the parade of frogs Rana led. Children cheered as they walked by, though they clearly thought the frogs belonged to Skyler, not Rana, dressed as Rana was in her punk-rock outfit from the dance.

"They don't know Skyler's a fake," Rana whispered to the frog prince on her shoulder. "And they don't know all these frogs are magic."

"We're not magic," said Sebastian. "We're *cursed*. That's different."

"How is it different?"

"A curse happens *to* you," Sebastian explained. "Magic is something you do."

"But if you curse someone, isn't that *doing* something?" asked Rana.

"Hmm." Sebastian thought. "I guess so. But it's the curser who does the magic, not the cursed. So, in this case, it's the witch who is magic, not me. Er . . ." He looked around at the colony of frogs hopping through the amusement park with them. "Us, I mean."

What he'd said started to give Rana an idea. When facing a magical problem, maybe you needed a magical solution.

"Excuse me! Trish!" Skyler approached a girl who looked exactly like Cindy, except she was dressed for a ball in a gleaming blue gown, studded with jewels, and her coils of black hair were tied up like a crown. A delicate diamond tiara was perched in her hair, and her dark skin shimmered like it had been dusted with glitter.

"How might I help you, my darling?" the princess said in a singsong voice that made Rana's nose wrinkle. The real Cindy radiated royalty, even if she was just wearing sweatpants. This princess was simply trying too hard.

The moment the nearest children were out of earshot, she dropped out of character. "What is it, Skyler?"

"I'm going on break," said Skyler.

"But it's ten minutes to closing!" said the pretend Cindy.

"I just have to get these frogs put away."

Cindy/Trish looked at the frogs and looked at Rana, suddenly registering how very strange it all was.

"I'm the wrangler," Rana offered quickly.

The other girl smiled and then turned to take a picture with some little children who had approached her with wide-eyed wonder. For all these kids knew, this Cinderella was completely real and excited to meet them. In fact, as she bent down to talk to them, her brown skin gleaming beneath the neon lights, her blue gown sparkling, she seemed to become Cindy for an instant. It was like watching a transformation spell. Maybe kids in this world had magic. They made this Cinderella real by believing she was real. What was Trish if not yet one more fractured fairy tale?

Leaving the pretend Cinderella behind, Skyler led them to the end of the Boulevard of Make-Believe. They turned left at the Magic Wand Emporium and Gift Shop, skirted around the Cursed Carousel and Fairy Fun Zone, and reached the entrance to the Woods of Wishes.

A rope stretched across the entrance, indicating it was closed, but Skyler ducked right underneath.

"My well is just up this way," said Skyler. "We can talk there in private."

Skyler's well was nothing like the well where Rana had met the frog prince. For one thing, there was a huge neon sign over it that read, "The Frog's Well," and for another, the trees around it were made of plastic and hid electric lights. Robotic owls hooted on a timer from the plastic branches. There was a fake mist on the ground, pumped out by machines, and the water in the well smelled of chlorine.

Skyler perched on the edge of it, took the plastic frog off her shoulder, and looked giddily at Rana and her many, many frogs. "Okay, so I cannot believe I'm meeting you! I'm such a fan! Tell me, are you from Faerie? Far Far Away? Long Long Ago?"

"Once Upon a Time," said Rana cautiously. "How did you know who I am?"

"Oh! Once Upon a Timers!" Skyler cheered. "Amazing! The real prince and princess from 'Der Froschkönig oder Der eiserne Heinrich'! I can't believe it!"

"Excuse me, what was that?" Rana asked. "Der Frosh Cone ick?"

"Oh sorry," said Skyler. "That's the title of 'The Frog Prince' in the original German. I learned German so I could read the original. You know, I've always loved fairy tales. That's why I work here. I'm kind of obsessed. I have twenty-seven editions of *Grimm's Fairy Tales* and all the movies and every retelling you can imagine. I have like sixty fairy-tale podcasts on my phone, even the grimmest ones! I mean . . . I'm sorry, do you know what a podcast is?"

"Yeah," said Rana. "I go to school just up the road."

"Of course!" said Skyler. "That place with the big gate, right? I couldn't be sure, but part of me just knew there was something up with that school! Is it for fairy-tale princesses?"

"Not exclusively," said Rana. "There are a few princes there too."

Skyler nearly fell into the well, she was so excited.

Rana reminded her to breathe, then pressed her. "But how did you recognize *me*?"

"Fairy tales are all I think about," said the girl. "I've always dreamed of being part of one. This amusement park is the closest I could get . . . until now! I mean, I dress up like you every day, but I knew you were the real you the moment I saw you at the gate. It was like *destiny*, like seeing yourself in the mirror for the first time. I just knew. I'm . . ." She smiled and curtsied to Rana. "I'm honored to meet you, Your Highness."

"Just call me Rana," she said.

"Rana! Of course, from the Latin for frog!" Skyler grinned.

"Exactly!" Prince Sebastian pumped a little frog fist in the air. "That's what I was telling her!"

Skyler's eyes nearly popped out of her head. "He just talked . . . I mean . . . of course . . . but he really talked! He's . . . is he . . . ? I mean . . . are they all . . . ? Why are there so many of them?"

"That," Rana told her, "is kind of why I'm here. They're fractured tales. They shouldn't be here."

"Neither should you!" one of them said.

"Come back with me and *I'll* be the original!" another said.

"My Rana thought *she* was original," said one more, sadly. "Before the After got her."

A chorus of *So did mine*s and *Mine too*s erupted.

Astonished, Skyler looked between the frogs, but Rana waited them out. "They do this," she said. "It's very annoying."

"I imagine it's hard for them to be frogs when they used to be princes," said Skyler.

"*She* really gets me," said Sebastian.

"That's good, because I need you to stay with her," said Rana. "All of you. I think you'll be safe here."

"With *me*?" Skyler said. "All of *them*?"

"Are you ready to be part of a dangerous quest to save a fairy tale?" Rana asked.

"Of course!" said Skyler. "But . . . why is it dangerous?"

"Because of the After," said Rana.

"What's an After?"

"It's nothing."

"Then why is it dangerous?"

"No, I mean it's literally nothing," said Rana. "It's like a nothing that creates more nothing. If it gets its hands on someone from our world, well . . . we become nothing."

"Oh," said Skyler. "That doesn't sound good."

"It's not," said Rana. "Do you think you can protect these princes from that?"

"I swear on every ever after I ever longed after," said Skyler, which was just the sort of jumbled mouthful that made for a good oath.

Rana smiled. "You have my thanks."

"You're not staying with us?" Sebastian asked anxiously.

"I can't," said Rana. "Someone has to figure out how to stop the After."

"It should be me!" said Sebastian, ever chivalrous.

"Or me!"

"Or me!" added all the others.

Rana shook her head. "You're frogs. And anyway, you helped already. You gave me the idea where I need to go."

"Where?"

"To the witch who cursed you," she said. "Like you said, *she* did the magic in our story, so she might know all about the After and how to stop it. If we don't have magic ourselves, we're going to need to use somebody else's."

"But that means going back to the story," said her frog prince. "And you said you never would."

He was right, and she definitely didn't *want* to go back. But sometimes even punk princesses had to do things they didn't want to do.

"I won't stay long," she said. "The sooner I get there, get this witch to help us, and get rid of the After, the sooner everything can go back to the way it should be."

"But what about us?" asked the other frogs. "The Rana in our versions of the story were de-storied. What are we supposed to do? Be stuck as frogs forever?"

She looked at them all without any answers. She wasn't sure she *could* solve their problem. In a story, the hero's plan could save everyone and set right all that had gone wrong. But in the real world, things that happened couldn't be fixed. Not every problem had a solution.

But that didn't mean she couldn't try.

"I'll see what I can do," she said, and then told the entire colony of frogs, "I'll be back for you soon. I promise."

"How will you get back into your fairy tale?" Skyler asked. "Are there, like, secret spells or magical portals?"

"Kind of," said Rana, closing her eyes to summon her way back. It took concentration and courage and she wasn't sure if she'd succeed. She'd never actually tried it before.

Skyler's scream told her when it worked.

When Rana opened her eyes, there in front of them was a huge monster with the legs of a man, the body and head of a frog, and a jagged iron crown on its head. When Rana nodded, it knelt, opened its mouth, and let its tongue unroll across the ground like a sticky red carpet.

"This is an Uponatime," said Rana. "And it's going to take me home."

CHAPTER NINE
Once Upon a Second Time

Uponatimes were the portals between the fairy-tale world and the real world. Each story had its own, and they seemed fearsome and ferocious, until you faced them, the way Rosamund had taught all the princesses to do. After facing them, they still *looked* fearsome and ferocious, but, it turned out, they were merely Doors of Opportunity. DOs were ways to return to your story when you were ready to *do* something. Nothing to fear if you were ready to look your story straight in the eye.

Rana did not feel ready to look her story straight in the eye, but the Uponatime had arrived, and the After was out there somewhere, and she had to do something. She had to go back whether she was ready or not.

It's just for a little while, she told herself. *Not forever. Or ever after. I'm just going to find the witch, learn how to stop the After, and return here, to my* real *life. That's all. No one is making me. I'm* choosing *to. This is* my *decision.*

Her little pep talk, however, had failed to make her feet move.

More than any frog-headed monster or shadowy After, Rana feared the world she'd come from, with its high walls, its endless rules, and its crushing loneliness. She feared the kind of person that world had made her, and she feared being trapped in that life again.

"Amazing!" Skyler gasped, peering into the Uponatime's mouth, which was now an open door. "It's the most beautiful place I've ever seen."

Skyler was not at all afraid of what she saw, though the sight chilled Rana to the bone. It was her bedroom in the castle, with its large canopy bed carved in intricate patterns from one giant tree. There were silk tapestries on the walls showing unicorns and butterflies and glorious sunrises. The tall windows around the room were flung open for a view of the floral meadows around the castle, where the sun was setting in brilliant reds and oranges and purples.

"It's like a scene from a fairy tale," said Skyler, and Rana gave her a side-eye. "Oh right," the girl squealed. "It *is!*"

"What's wrong, Princess?" Sebastian asked Rana. "You look frightened of your own bedroom."

"I'm not afraid of anything," she told him. Even though everyone could see that she was, literally, at this exact moment, shaking in her boots.

"I can accompany you, my princess," Sebastian offered from his perch on Skyler's palm.

"Me too!" Skyler added enthusiastically.

Rana shook her head. "The witch who turned you into a frog probably won't be keen on helping you out now, would she?"

The frog looked down, but said no more.

"I can do this," she told them. "I'll see you all very soo—" She froze. Her face went white as a new tooth, and her mouth opened without sound. But it wasn't from magic. It was older and more powerful than any spell.

It was terror.

A shadow had risen behind Skyler and stood faceless and silent, arms outstretched on either side of her head.

The After had found them after all. Sebastian hopped from her palm like a . . . well, like a frog leaping to safety, which is precisely what he was.

He and the other frogs huddled and shivered on the far side of the fake well.

Skyler whirled around to look at the shadow.

"Be careful!" Rana warned Skyler as the After closed its arms around her in a bear hug. Instead of grabbing her, it passed right through her body. It stopped on the other side of Skyler, and its inhuman head cocked. Rana thought it seemed confused. *How does nothing get confused?* she wondered.

While Skyler didn't vaporize the way the princes at the dance had, she was not unaffected by the shadow passing through her. Her eyes lost their focus. She looked distant and dulled.

"Everyone looks so worried," she said. "What's wrong?"

"Um? The After? The giant living shadow? Right in front of you?" said Sebastian.

Skyler's eyes focused on the giant living shadow right in front of her, but instead of screaming or running, she just shrugged. "I don't suppose it matters. All this is silly anyway. I should go back to work."

"What's happened to her?" one of the frogs cried.

"The After," Rana said. "Maybe when a real-world person is de-storied, it means that they're drained of all wonder and curiosity and personality and will. Even in this world, a person without a story is hardly a person at all."

"We have to help her!" said Sebastian.

Rana agreed. This girl had been ready to help them, strangers though they were to her, and they owed her the same kindness.

"When I say go, all frogs hop to the left," she told them. "Hopefully, the After will follow you and I'll be able to grab Skyler."

"We're ready!" the chorus of frog princes shouted. Maybe there was more to these little frog boys than she'd always assumed.

"Go!" she yelled.

All the frogs, except Sebastian, leaped to the left, and the After followed the sudden movement. Rana jumped to the right, grabbing Skyler with her free hand and pulling her away from the After. Toward the giant Uponatime's mouth.

"What's this about?" asked Skyler, sounding more bored than afraid. At least a de-storied person was easy to drag around. Take away someone's story and you could make them do anything.

"We're going where you've always dreamed of going," said Rana.

She pulled the girl up the frog creature's tongue as the After hesitated between the frogs and the princesses, unsure which one to pursue.

"Can you even do that?" asked Sebastian. "Bring a real-world person into our fairy tale?"

"We came into their world," said Rana. "Why shouldn't it work the other way too?"

"Because the real world is strange and mysterious," said Sebastian. "In fairy tales, there are rules!"

"I've never cared for rules," said Rana as she pulled Skyler through the portal into her bedroom, her frog prince hopping from her palm onto her shoulder to keep a lookout.

"The After's coming after us!" he shouted.

The After moved toward them as the Uponatime's mouth began to close.

"We'll hold it off for you!" another frog shouted. "Just find a way to destroy it before *it* de-stories the rest of us!"

"I will! I promise!" Rana called back, though she wasn't

sure they'd heard her before the Door of Opportunity closed completely. That was probably for the best, as she had no idea if she'd be able to keep that promise.

"What now?" asked Sebastian from atop a velvet cushioned bench at the end of her grand bed.

The portal was gone, and Rana was back in her dreaded bedchamber, except this time, Skyler was with her, dressed as a princess, while she was still dressed as a punk rocker, and Prince Sebastian was still a frog.

"You were a prince when I left," she told him.

"But my curse was never broken," he said. "*Because* you left."

"I should go find that witch right away," Rana said.

"I still think I should go with you," said Prince Sebastian. "What am I supposed to do while you're wandering in the dark woods?"

One glance out the window showed Rana that the woods were indeed very dark. If the After did find a way back here, she wouldn't see it coming until it was too late.

"Keep an eye on her, I guess?" Rana suggested, and they both looked at Skyler, standing dazed in the middle of the royal bedroom.

"Is this . . . am I . . . ," she asked, glassy-eyed.

"In a fairy tale, yes," said Rana. "'The Frog Prince,' to be precise," she added. "Although I really don't know why it's called that, when it's *my* story."

"It's my story," croaked Prince Sebastian under his frog breath. "But whatever."

"Where's your servant?" Rana asked, looking out the window. "Maybe he can keep a lookout for us?"

"After you left, he went searching the woods for you," said the prince. "I never saw him again. That's why I followed you when I finally found a way to the Academy. I was lonely."

Rana felt bad about that. She couldn't imagine what it was like to be turned into a frog *and then* to lose your best friend in the world.

Then again, she'd left all her friends behind at the HEA to come back here, so maybe she *could* imagine something like what he had felt.

They looked at one another without speaking, the princess and the frog, and for a moment, it seemed they both understood each other perfectly.

For that same moment it looked like Skyler still didn't

remember her dream of being a fairy-tale princess, but then her smiled bloomed like a thousand roses.

"I can't believe it!" She rushed to the window and gazed out over the deep, dark woods. "A castle! A royal bedroom! An enchanted forest!" She spun around. "A handsome frog prince!"

"Well, yes, I am." The frog puffed up his chest.

Rana rolled her eyes. "I thought we'd lost you to the After," she said.

"It felt like you had," Skyler told them. "Terrible. I felt so empty, so tired. I couldn't think straight and didn't want to. It was like I'd fallen into a deep well. I could see the sky, but had no way to reach it. The walls were slippery and smooth. But coming here . . . seeing this? It helped me climb back to myself."

"The After passed right through you," said Rana. "I wonder what would've happened if it had held on."

"I might have fallen deeper than even my dreams could rescue me from," Skyler said.

"Okay, well, you two stay put," Rana instructed them. "Don't come out of this room. And don't let my parents see you."

"They already know I'm here," said the frog prince.

"Right." Rana remembered. Her parents had forced her to let the frog up to her room in the first place. "Well, just stay in here and they'll think we're both here. I'm gonna go find this witch and see if she can help us stop the After before it's too late."

"How do you do that?" asked Sebastian. "How do you find a witch? You know she's a minor character, right?"

"It's one of the first rules of fairy tales," Skyler explained to him. "The minor characters appear just when you need them. As long as you're in the right place and desperate enough."

"But Rana doesn't like rules," the prince said.

"Well, I'll do what I have to do to save us," said Rana. "Even if that means playing by the rules."

"Do you know where the right place is?" asked Prince Sebastian.

"Of course," said Rana. She looked at Skyler to explain. The girl knew fairy tales better than Rana ever would.

"The woods. It's always the woods," Skyler said.

Rana was already out the door.

CHAPTER TEN
One Foot in Front of the Other

Since the dawn of time and the start of all stories, whenever a fairy-tale character needed something to happen, for good or ill, they went into the woods. The woods were where magic lurked, and danger and destiny too.

"In the real world, it's nothing but ticks," Rana said to herself, letting the sound of her own voice comfort her as the moonlight grew dimmer, blotted out by the thick canopy of trees overhead.

The deeper she went, the dimmer it got, and the more she needed courage. She thought about her friends back at school, about how just being among the brave princesses of the Academy gave her courage. She wished they were with her now, but even without them, she kept walking, one foot in front of the other into the dark. One foot in front of the other, though wolves howled in the distance. One foot in front of the other, though she nearly jumped out of her skin at every shadow. One foot in front of the other, no matter how scared she was, and that was pretty much the same thing as courage.

Still, she felt the need to talk to herself.

"I wonder what they're doing at school right now?" she asked. "Snack homework? Fencing? Forming a search committee?"

The thought made her sad, but also happy at the same time. Here in her story, no one missed her. No one even really knew her. Not her servants, not her family, not even Prince Sebastian or Skyler.

"I'm a stranger here," she said. "Would anyone notice if I disappeared in these woods for good?"

"I'd notice!" the frog prince said from behind her. She whirled around, and there he sat, a lump on a leaf, looking up with hope and expectation, like always.

"I told you not to follow me!" she scolded. "Where's Skyler?"

"She stayed behind at the castle," said the frog. "She's never been in a real castle before."

"You should go back to keep an eye on her," Rana told him. "For your own good as much as hers!"

"My own good is wherever you are, princess," Prince Sebastian said back.

"It's not safe for you out here."

"It's not safe *for you* out here! You're a princess in the woods. I'm a frog. Frogs live in the woods."

"You're a prince," she said.

"But no one else knows that," he said.

"The witch does."

"The witch can bite my toes." Sebastian scoffed. "I eat witches for breakfast."

"Go home," she told him. "This is my quest and I'm doing it alone. If I have to snatch you up and carry you back to the castle in my pocket," she told him. "I will."

"Just try it," he said.

"Fine." She took a step toward him.

He hopped away.

She stepped toward him again.

He hopped away again.

"Stop it," she said.

"Make me," he said.

"I will."

Step, hop, step. They went on like that for a while, the

frog always just out of Rana's reach.

Step, hop, step.

"You're wasting time," said the frog.

"You're the one wasting time," said Rana. "Go back so I can get on with finding the witch."

"Why do you want to do this all yourself?" he asked.

"Because I *have* to," she said. "I'm tired of other people making the events of my story—of my *life*—happen. I have to be the one who makes my story happen. Me."

"All I hear is *me me me*," said the frog prince. "It's very selfish."

"It's very *un*-selfish!" said Rana. "I'm protecting you by making you leave!"

They were on the edge of a small pond. She saw the prince's eyes dart to the water.

"Don't you dare," she told him.

And then, with a plop, the frog prince was off, into the water, leaping from lily pad to lily pad. Rana went splashing in after him.

"Come back here and let me save you!" she yelled.

But whenever she got close, he dove under the water and splurched through the mud. Other frogs, regular old forest frogs, watched from their perches and lily pads and hidey-holes, only jumping away when Rana got too close.

She belly flopped on top of Sebastian, soaked and stinking of pond scum. But she came up with her hands full. "Gotcha!"

"No need to bring innocents into this!" the frog prince called from a rock just by Rana's foot.

The little frog in her hand shuddered and stared with amphibian terror. It was the wrong size and the wrong color.

She dropped the poor frog she'd caught and lunged after the correct one, who swam away faster than she could grab him. They circled and dove and splashed for ages. Every time Rana got close, the frog prince skittered from her.

"You really shouldn't grab a frog barehanded," he said. "Salmonella!"

"Salmon is a fish!" Rana countered.

"Salmonella is a dangerous bacteria you can get from handling reptiles! Remember science class at our school?"

"It's *my* school!" Rana yelled, and lunged. He plunged under the water and popped his head up just out of reach. "And there's no salmonella in fairy tales."

"Thank goodness for that," the frog said. "Can you

imagine a dragon with indigestion?"

Rana couldn't help smirking. Professor Perrault had indigestion all the time in his human form.

"Or a knight with the runs?" the prince added. "All that armor to take off in a hurry!"

Rana laughed, imagining what passing gas would sound like inside a suit of armor. The laughter melted her anger.

"Everyone would pretend the king's flatulence smelled like roses," she said.

"Fetch the royal retching bowl!" the frog joked, making Rana laugh harder.

"The princely puke bucket!" he declared.

Even though she stood knee-deep in a muddy pond in a deep, dark wood, Rana was laughing so hard she could cry. The frog prince too laughed in his croaking way. She found when he wasn't trying to make her do something she didn't want to, he was kind of fun. That didn't make her love him, but it did make her *like* him.

"When you're not acting like a pushy fairy-tale frog, you're not so bad," she told him with a smile.

"And when you're not acting like a spoiled princess, you're not so bad yourself," he said.

"All we had to do to become friends was chase each other into a pond." Rana laughed.

"And make some disgusting jokes about bowel movements," added the prince.

This set them both to laughing again. Rana doubled over, almost cackling.

Actually, in fact, cackling.

Is that really how I laugh? she asked herself and stopped laughing altogether.

The cackling, however, continued. High-pitched and bone-chilling.

She looked up, and the frog prince was gone, not even a ripple in the pond where he had been.

And there at the edge of the water, standing in a sliver of silver moonlight between two alder trees, stood the witch.

"Lost in a pond, little dearie?" the witch called out, mischief in her tone. "Lost your wits, I think, laughing to yourself in the muck all alone."

Rana felt a moment of relief. The witch thought Rana was alone, which meant Sebastian had hidden safely, at least for now.

"Come out of the pond, child," the witch told her. "You

can dry off in my cottage. It's hardly a castle fit for a princess, but you're hardly a princess fit for a castle, are you?"

The witch cackled again and walked off, beckoning Rana to follow.

One foot in front of the other, she told herself, mustering every scrap of courage she could find. She followed the witch deeper into the woods, which was never a good idea in a fairy tale.

CHAPTER ELEVEN
What's with You and Frogs?

The cottage was cozier than she'd expected a witch's woodland lair to be, but between frog princes and plastic princess parks, Rana had learned not to make assumptions based on appearances. A cozy lair could hide unimaginable dangers, just as a plastic park filled with pretend princesses could contain heroes worthy of any fairy tale.

"What brings you here, Princess Rana?"

"How do you know who I am?" asked Rana, who was still dressed in her punk-rock outfit from the school dance, though caked with mud and pond scum. The witch just gestured at her, like, *duh*. "Never mind. I need to know why the After is after us. Why is it de-storying everything from my story?"

"*Your* story?" said the witch. "Why do you think it's your story? It's not even named after you."

"It's 'The Frog Prince,' I know," said Rana. "But I'm the one it's about."

"Are you sure?" The witch smiled without a shred of kindness on her lips. She threw some carrots into the cauldron with a bubbly splash. "Get to the point! I'm very busy."

"Making a potion?" asked Rana.

"Making my dinner!" snapped the witch. "Who ever heard of putting carrots in a potion? *Pah!*"

The witch spat on the dirt floor of her own house. "All you royals are the same. Spoiled brats who only think of yourselves, never of the little people. *That's* why I turned that Prince Sebastian into a frog. To teach him some humility. And it looks like you need to learn what humility is yourself!"

"I know what humility is!"

"And yet you still think this story is about *you*!" The witch reached for a gnarly old stick sitting on a shelf behind her. A magic wand! "I think you'd be better as a frog yourself. Hope you like jumping, little froggy!"

The tip of the wand glowed and sparkled with green light. Rana feared she was done for, when a "ribbit" from the windowsill drew the witch's attention away.

"Sebastian!" Rana cried out.

"You!" the witch shrieked. "What are you doing here?"

"Saving my princess!" Prince Sebastian declared as he leaped from the windowsill to the witch's table, knocking aside a potato or two in the process. Then he stopped himself and looked at Rana. "I mean . . . *my friend*."

"So she hasn't fallen in love with you yet? Ha! I guess you'll be a frog forever." The witch cackled. "I can't blame her! I don't know what that Heinrich boy sees in you!"

"I think I'm starting to charm her," Prince Sebastian said. "Just because I'm a frog, doesn't mean I can't—"

"Wait!" Rana interrupted. "What was that about Heinrich?"

"Nothing." The witch raised her wand again.

"How do you know Sebastian's servant?"

"Forget I said anything!" said the witch as Sebastian flicked his frog tongue at the soup she had cooking, trying to get a taste. "And you! Stop tonguing my food! Once I turn Rana into a frog, perhaps I'll make myself some froggy stew out of both of you! That'll—*ah!*"

While the witch had been distracted, Rana had snatched the wand from her hand and yanked it away. Then she pointed it straight at the witch's heart.

"How dare you snatch a witch's wand!" The witch took a step toward her. Rana waved the wand in what felt like a threatening way. "You've no idea how to use it."

Rana felt cold sweat race down her back. Of course she had no idea how to use the wand. She'd acted without thinking, like always.

But what she had was a gut feeling. And when all else failed, her guts had to be enough.

"You're right. I don't know how to use it." She grabbed one end of the wand in each fist, preparing to snap it. "But I can destroy it."

The witch froze. Her eyes looked wide as a frog's. "You wouldn't dare."

"Maybe I wouldn't," she said. "If you tell me how you know Heinrich."

The witch scowled. "Why wouldn't I know him? His name's in the title of the story."

"Don't be silly," croaked Sebastian.

The witch narrowed her eyes. "You're lucky the girl has my wand, little hopper, or I'd be having frog's legs for dinner."

Sebastian gulped.

The witch looked back at Rana. "You probably didn't know that the full title of this story is 'The Frog Prince or Iron Heinrich.'"

"What?" Sebastian gasped. "Why's my servant in the title of *my* story?"

But Rana was starting to figure it out. "You were right. It really isn't my story," Rana told him. "But it's not exactly *yours* either."

"You think this is about Heinrich?" Sebastian marveled. "But he's hardly in the story at all!"

"Tell us about him," Rana demanded of the witch. "Why is he in the title?"

"You never got to the end. You don't know a thing about him," said the witch.

"Can he help me stop the After?"

"You can't stop the After," the witch told her. "It's a void. A nothing. And all it wants is to be filled. It will swallow everything in its path, trying to fill the nothing inside itself."

"Did it swallow Heinrich?" Sebastian asked. "Or did you turn him into a frog too?"

"He begged me to turn him into a frog, you know." She examined her fingernails as she spoke. "He came to see me and pleaded that whatever had happened to you should happen to him too."

"He was a loyal servant," said Sebastian, sniffling. "And a good friend."

"Friendship is as deep a well of love as romance," scoffed the witch. "Maybe deeper. And you ignored it. You ignored him. Pitiful."

Sebastian drooped.

"Did you grant his wish?" Rana asked.

"Of course not. I don't grant wishes. I do curses. It's my whole thing."

"Then what are you good for?" Sebastian croaked.

"I don't have to be *good* for anything," said the witch. "My job isn't to be good. It's to be the witch! But I did Heinrich an even better bit of magic," she continued. "He wept from a broken heart, so I mended it, in my own way. I took three iron—*erp!*"

She stopped short, startled.

"Three iron erp?" asked the frog prince. "What's an erp?"

The witch didn't answer. Instead, she took a frightened step backward, bumping into her cauldron, and pointed at the wall behind Rana.

Rana spun just as the giant shadow stepped from the lighter shadows and towered over the cottage. A void in space where, a moment before, the cottage door had stood firmly shut.

The thing reached out its empty arms, like it wanted to hug all three of them in a terrible embrace.

"Ah!" Rana yelled. She leaped backward beside the witch and the frog prince and raised the witch's wand.

"You don't know how to use that! You're not a witch!" cried the witch.

But it was too late. Rana gestured as magically as she could think to, and an explosion of green goo erupted from the wand's tip. Just like the blast of Mentos and soda at the dance, it burst out in every direction . . . every direction except her target.

The goo smashed into an iron ladle hanging on the wall, which turned into an iron frog and clattered to the floor. The goo coated two wooden chairs at Rana's side, and they both turned into wooden frogs. A painting on the wall of a woman stirring a cauldron turned into a painting of a frog stirring a cauldron.

The last blob splattered the witch herself. Her eyes went

wide and her mouth fell open. She looked a little sickly green, and then a lot sickly green. Her skin bubbled, her eyes kept bulging, and, with a wet-sounding "POP," she turned into a large warty toad.

"What is it with you and frogs?" Sebastian wondered aloud.

"You little brute! Turn me back!" the frog witch croaked, but Rana looked down at the wand in her hands, which had turned to moss and crumbled between her fingers. The witch saw it at the same time Rana did, then looked at the After, drifting closer.

"Forget you! I'm going to a tale where I'm appreciated!" she said. With that, she took a giant froggy leap straight into the air, then, tilting her body down, put her front legs together and splashed headfirst into her soup.

Just like that, she was gone.

Rana and the frog prince rushed to the brim of the cauldron and looked in. Where once there had been soup, they saw a long water slide, the frog witch sliding down it among the chunks of carrots and potatoes. "See ya never!" she yelled back at them, and then the soup bubbled up once more, and whatever doorway the witch had taken was gone.

"What did she just do?"

"I think that was her Door of Opportunity," said Rana.

"What are *we* supposed to do?"

"What I always do," said Rana. "Run!"

She snatched up the little frog and scurried out the window before the After could get its annihilating arms around them.

When she hit the forest floor, Rana didn't stop. She ran from the hut, trying to put as much distance between herself and the monster as she could.

"How did it follow us here?" Sebastian wondered. "It's like it's drawn to us wherever we are, no matter what world we're in."

"Not us," Rana said. "You. I think it's drawn to you."

"But why?"

"Heinrich," she said. "Heinrich is the key."

Sebastian shook his head. "But he's a—"

"A minor character?" Rana raised an eyebrow.

"Yeah," said Sebastian.

"I guess there is no such thing, is there?" Rana noted.

"Maybe you shouldn't have ditched him to chase after me?"

"Guess not," agreed Sebastian. "I mean, he was my friend, but . . . I'm the prince. I'm supposed to pursue the princess, not, like, hang out with my friend."

"The witch was right," said Rana. "Friendship is as deep a well of love as romance. A friend can know you better than anyone in the world."

As she said it, she thought about how much she missed her own friends back at the Academy.

Sebastian sniffled and wiped his little frog nose with his little frog forearm. "But without the witch, we have no idea what's happened to Heinrich."

"We can find out," said Rana. "Who knows this story better than anyone?"

"Skyler!" Sebastian cheered.

"She'll tell us what happened to Heinrich. I know he's the key. He's missing and the story has a blank space without him. A void."

"Whoa," said Prince Sebastian. "You're, like, wildly smart."

"I know," said Rana. "But thanks. And also . . . thanks for stopping the witch from enfroggening me too."

"My pleasure," he said.

"This one time," she told him. "I'm glad you followed me."

"I'd follow you anywhere, m'lady," said the frog prince with as much romance as his voice could muster. "Sorry," he muttered. "Just a habit."

They ran through the dark woods together, firmly friends now, and it felt good. She'd hate to seem him de-storied just as they were getting to know one another.

So she ran faster for the castle and hoped Skyler knew as much about fairy tales as she claimed to.

CHAPTER TWELVE
Hitting a Wall

They raced inside the castle, startling the guards and the servants alike, who jumped out of the way of the black-clad princess with a chorus of gasps and a clattering of dishes.

"Sorry," she called back over her shoulder to them as she ran, which she realized might've been the first time she'd ever spoken to the servants. She'd never thought of them as characters that mattered before. But if she'd been wrong about Heinrich, she could probably be wrong about any of them.

For a moment, she had the urge to turn back and speak to each of them, to ask them about their lives and their hopes and their fears. But then she remembered the shadow chasing her and the frog prince, and that it would de-story them all if she didn't stop it soon, so she kept running, racing for the stairs to her bedroom to find Skyler.

Except Skyler wasn't in the bedroom. Rana nearly tripped over her own feet, stopping short in the door to one of the seventeen sitting rooms in the castle, one that was usually dark and unused.

It was now brightly lit and her parents were sitting in it, laughing boisterously, which was not something Rana could recall them ever doing before. There was a rule against boisterous laughter. There was a rule against boisterous anything, actually.

Sitting on the satin couch across from her parents was Skyler, who must have just said something to have ignited the king and queen's laughter.

As one, they turned to look at Rana, out of breath, panting in the doorway.

"Ah, darling, you're here!" Her father waved her over. "We wondered where you had been. We've just been chatting with your delightful friend!"

"My . . . um . . ." Rana was speechless. Her parents had never described anyone but her as delightful before and had never let her have friends at all. And now, Skyler was both! *How?*

"Don't let your mouth hang open like a fallen drawbridge," her mother scolded. "You could take a manners lesson from your friend!"

"And what *are* you wearing?" her father asked, sizing up her black outfit of jeans and T-shirt. Perfect sneaking-around-on-an-adventure clothes, but not at all something a princess should wear.

"That is not at all something a princess should wear!" He gestured out of the room, to the grand staircase. "Go change into something proper at once."

"But I *like* what I'm wearing," Rana answered him. "I don't have time to argue with you right now. I need to talk to my friend in private right away."

Now her father's mouth hung open like a fallen drawbridge. Perfect princesses did not talk back to their parents. That was certainly against the rules.

"I'm not sure I heard you," her mother said with a steely smile. "Did you say you aren't sure which dress to choose? You have so many, after all. I understand how it would be difficult to decide. I'm sure your friend Skyler could help you. Her kingdom sounds like a wonderful place."

"Her kingdom?" Rana bulged her eyes at Skyler, who

returned an almost imperceptible shrug. Rana shook her head before yelling at her parents. "I don't need help deciding what dress to wear! I am happy with what I'm wearing now! These clothes are *me*!"

"They are certainly *not*!" her father yelled back at her. "You are a princess and you will dress like one!"

"Go to your room!" her mother snapped. "Now!"

Rana hesitated. She wanted to yell right back at her parents that she would *not* go to her room and that she didn't have to follow their rules anyway! But, also, the sooner she got away from her parents, the safer they would be.

"I'm going," she snapped. "But *not* because you told me to."

She stomped off. Sebastian still clung to his hiding place under her hair.

"I'll go talk to her," Skyler said to her parents, which made Rana even madder.

Not even one night back in her story and already she was being told what to wear and what to do. This was everything she had feared and every reason that she had fled her story in the first place.

The moment Skyler entered her room, Rana whirled on

her. "This isn't some game you get to just jump in and play. This is my life."

"The life you left," Skyler reminded her.

"It's still mine!" she said. "How did you get them to like you so much? They never think anyone is good enough for me."

"Easy," said Skyler. "I just acted like they think *you* should. They loved it."

"You're the perfect princess they always wanted me to be," Rana said.

"They know you're unhappy, by the way," Skyler explained. "They just don't know how to help. They really do mean well."

"You discussed me?" Rana asked.

"Of course we did," said Skyler. "What else could we have talked about? They were worried sick when you disappeared."

"When I . . . oh right." When Rana left her story, she'd left them too. She'd never even considered their feelings.

But when the other girls in the Princess Protection Program fled their stories, their stories had stopped. Everyone just sort of existed, anxiously biding their time until something important could happen again, like in a dentist's waiting room.

But her story had kept going in her absence.

Because it isn't my story. It never was. It didn't stop until Sebastian left to find me, she realized.

And that was the same time, she figured, the After appeared, trying to find him.

"I need you to tell us the story of Iron Heinrich," Rana told Skyler. "As quickly as you can."

"Iron Heinrich?" she said. "But that's *your* story. Don't you know your own story?"

"Not the ending," said Rana, glancing at the door. "Please hurry."

"Okay, well . . . let's see . . . the frog helps you recover your golden ball from the well, and then you leave him in the woods. He follows you home and—"

"We know this part," said Rana. "Skip to the end. With Heinrich."

"Oh okay," she said, thinking. "He's kind of a weird character. He's never explained and a lot of versions of the tale leave him out entirely. But after you throw the prince at the wall and he becomes human and you kiss and fall in love, the servant is there to take you to the prince's castle."

"He's just there? Waiting?"

"Yes," said Skyler. "It's the first time he's even mentioned. Like he's just kind of attached to wherever the prince is."

"Told you," said Prince Sebastian. "Loyalty."

Skyler kept going. "While you're riding home, you hear a loud clang that startles you both. Then another. Then another. Three clangs. You worry the carriage has broken an axle, but Heinrich says that no, that's him. When the prince turned into a frog, his heart broke. So he had three iron bands placed around it to hold his heart together."

"The witch!" Rana exclaimed. "She placed those iron bands on his heart!"

"Did she tell you that?" Skyler asked.

"Yeah, before I accidentally . . . never mind. Keep going," said Rana.

"Heinrich's heart is so filled with joy that his prince is finally back that the iron bands break and his heart is free again. That's how the story ends. None of it's really explained though. I'm not even sure I understand it."

"But I do," said Rana. "The witch put the iron bands

around his heart so he wouldn't feel sad, but a heart of iron can't feel anything at all. No pain, but no happiness either. Nothing. It's . . . a void."

"So Heinrich *is* the After!" Sebastian cried out.

"That explains why he's drawn to you no matter where you go," said Rana. "He wants you back, trying to fill the void in himself with anything he can, but nothing will ever be enough. Like a black hole, it sucks in all the light. It doesn't mean to; it just can't stop."

"So how do we stop it?" asked Sebastian.

"We have to unbreak his heart," Rana said.

"Like . . . if I was human again?" Sebastian said. "That seems to be what he wanted."

"Worth a try," said Skyler.

"If you'd like to throw me at the wall, you can," Sebastian suggested. "Bonus is that I'd like to be human again myself."

Rana grabbed the little frog. He shut his eyes, bracing for the coming throw. She cranked her arm back and hesitated.

The frog opened one eye. "I'm ready," he said.

"Will this hurt you?" she asked.

"It didn't before. Well, not too badly."

Rana nodded. She swallowed hard and then threw the

frog at the wall. His little legs flew over his head, cartwheeling across the air until he hit the far wall with a wet thud.

He slid down to the floor, groaning, but as befrogged as before.

"It didn't work." He sighed. "Why didn't it work?"

"Maybe because I meant it last time," suggested Rana. "I was mad at you. But I can't fake it. I'm not mad at you this time."

"She's right," Skyler said. "You have to mean it. That's the whole thing with fairy tales. As unreal as the stories seem, the emotions are real. That's why the tales have lasted so long. You *are* people with real feelings."

"Of course we are!" said Rana.

"If you aren't mad at him," said Skyler, "maybe the other thing would work. From the other versions of your story?"

"What other thing?" Rana asked.

Prince Sebastian looked up from the floor and let out an excited "ribbit."

Rana wrinkled her nose. "Oh," she said. "A kiss."

"It might be our only hope," Sebastian said, a little too eagerly.

Rana's shoulders slumped and she trudged across the

room to pick him up. "I resent this," she said, before closing her eyes and planting a delicate kiss on the top of the slimy frog's head.

When she opened her eyes . . . he was still a frog.

"You didn't mean it," he said.

"Duh!"

"This is hopeless!' the frog cried out, hopping down onto the pillows of her bed. "We're doomed! If you can't fall in love with me, then we'll all be destroyed!"

"De-storied," Rana corrected.

"Whatever!" The little frog wept.

Rana sat down next to him. "I'm sorry. I really am. But I can't *make* myself feel something I just don't. And I can't force myself to stay here either. I'm not the princess my parents want, and I'm not the princess you need. I can't be. Skyler is right, faking it doesn't work. Our stories require our truth."

"Easy for you to say," the frog whined. "You weren't turned into a frog!"

"I was turned into someone I'm not," said Rana sadly. "The same as you. Though I had prettier clothes."

"Except you hate pretty clothes."

"True," Rana said. "But we have to do something here. We can't just sit around waiting for the After to de-story everyone. We have to act!"

"We don't have a plan," said the frog.

"That has never stopped me before," she told him. "One thing I refuse to do is put on a pretty dress and do nothing."

"You know, wearing a pretty dress doesn't stop you from doing things," Skyler said. "Some of the greatest women in history wore pretty dresses while changing the world. And guess what? Some of us actually *like* pretty dresses."

Rana felt a little embarrassed that she'd insulted Skyler's love of pretty dresses. The clothes, as she knew, don't make the magic. The person does.

"So . . . who has new ideas?" asked the frog. "And before you answer, you need to know this conversation has developed some urgency."

He pointed at the door. The After had caught up with them. It poured like ink through the keyhole and formed into the shape—Rana could now see it—of a boy. A large, hungry, brokenhearted, void boy.

And he reached out to grab them.

CHAPTER THIRTEEN
All's Well

"Heinrich! Stop!" Prince Sebastian croaked at the top of his tiny lungs. He hopped to the end of the bed, bravely staring down the shadowy creature that loomed before him.

And the shadow stopped. Rana watched it twist around itself, literally tying itself in knots as it looked at the frog.

"It's his name!" Rana cried out. "He's responding to hearing his name! It *is* him!"

"Heinrich, listen to me," said the prince, trying to sound calm and as human as his little frog voice could. "I know you're in there. I know you don't mean to hurt anyone, but every time you touch someone, they're de-storied. Do you understand?"

The edges of the creature that had been Heinrich wavered, that same confused tilt to its head.

"It's working," Rana urged. "Keep talking to him!"

"I know you want me back in my human form," the frog

prince told him. "Trust me, I want me back too. But I can't force Rana to change me. She can't fake it. We have to be . . . patient."

The shadow flickered. Then it reached one arm out, like a wisp of smoke drifting across the room. It tried to stroke the frog's head, but Sebastian jumped out of the way at the last moment.

"Heinrich! If you touch me, I'll disappear! You have to stop. Please!"

But the creature couldn't stop. Rana understood now. Sometimes, when she got angry, she lashed out at people who cared about her: her teachers, her friends, her family. Sometimes she broke rules just because she was told she shouldn't. She could be mean and bratty and defiant, and she could even see herself doing it and not be able to stop. Emotions were like a fire; they could warm you and give you light, or they could run out of control and burn up everything they touched. One of the reasons Rana liked punk rock was that it channeled her anger and turned it into art.

Heinrich had anger too. All people did. And he'd had truly terrible feelings when the prince transformed into a frog, but instead of dealing with a broken heart, crying or writing a sad song or a depressing poem or something, he bound his heart to make it feel nothing. When his prince left the story altogether, it must have been too much to bear. But a heart that couldn't break, couldn't heal.

So instead, it collapsed. It turned him into *this*. A hungry nothingness that he couldn't control. Some part of him might *want* to stop, but he just couldn't. The void demanded to be filled.

"Heinrich! It's me you want!" Rana yelled, grabbing the shadow's attention. "It's *my* fault your prince is still a frog! I'm the cause of all your pain!"

The shadow was hungry, but maybe not mindless. It understood, or seemed to. Maybe it wasn't just grief inside the darkness, but anger too. And that anger might be something they could use to survive.

The shadow oozed in her direction.

"Rana, what are you doing?" the prince asked.

"I'm buying us time," she said, leading the After in a loop of her room to clear the way to the door. "He'll follow me now."

"But . . . him following you is not exactly solving the

problem," said Skyler. The frog and the girl from the real world looked worriedly at each other.

"Don't be so nervous!" Rana reassured them. "I have a plan!"

With that, she turned and ran from room, hoping they hadn't heard the wavering of her voice, because, being honest, her only plan was to get the monster out of her bedroom. Her plan was to run.

That had always worked for her before. She'd run from her story once, after all, and had already run from the After a few times. And even back in her story, when the frog had made her promise to take him home, she'd run from him. Running, it seemed, was her main character trait.

This time, though, she was running *toward* something, not just away.

She'd been lucky that when she'd run from her story, she'd found a place that showed her other possibilities, other lives she could live. She'd seen that the life of the fairy-tale princess wasn't the only one for her.

She had changed her story. And maybe she could show Heinrich that he could change his too.

She wasn't about to lead him back to her school, but that witch had been more helpful than she'd meant to be. When she'd jumped away, she showed Rana that you could create a doorway anywhere.

And Rana knew just the place for a new doorway.

Luckily—or at least, what passed for luck right now—the thing followed her from her bedroom and kept following her through the castle, out a servant's entrance, through the courtyard, and to the open meadow that led back into the woods.

Behind her, Heinrich drifted as slow and steady as ever, giving his relentless chase.

She veered off as soon as she hit the tree line, sprinting down a path she'd been on before. Her feet carried her over rotten logs and gnarly roots. She ran past trees that looked like gnomes and mossy rocks that looked like trolls. She very nearly brained herself on a low branch when she was distracted by a murder of startled crows launching themselves into the air.

Why the woods were thick with fog on a pleasant night was anyone's guess. Rana figured it had something to do with fairy-tale magic, but now that she'd lived in a world with weather satellites and apps that could predict rain a week in advance, she wondered what sense it made to have fogs that came and went with the mood of the story.

She ran to the well.

The well where she first met the frog prince.

When the After caught up with her, she locked her eyes on it and smiled.

"Listen here, Heinrich," she said. "I can't fill the emptiness that's consumed you. No one can . . . except for you."

The monster didn't even waver. He just kept coming.

"If you don't like how your story goes, you can fracture it," she continued. "You just need a little help."

And with that, she climbed onto the stone edge of the old well, looked once more at the shadow, and dared it to follow her.

Okay, she thought. *This worked for the witch; I sure hope it works for me.*

Just as the After stretched out its impossibly long arms, she grabbed her nose to keep from inhaling a bunch of well water and jumped. She dropped into the well like her golden ball had before her, and hoped a Door of Opportunity would open somewhere below.

If it didn't, she was about to get very wet before she got erased from existence completely.

CHAPTER FOURTEEN
Fractured Frogs

The drop into the dark lasted longer than she'd imagined it could. *Surely there's water down here somewhere?* Up above, the light of the world narrowed and narrowed to the size of a small golden ball, then to a pinprick, then to nothing. She fell and fell and fell. She didn't know if the shadow had followed her, because everything was darkness now.

And still she fell.

In stories, leaps of faith are supposed to be rewarded, she thought. *But what if I was wrong? What if I am going to pay for my recklessness with falling for all eternity?*

She also thought: *At least if the After followed me, he'll fall forever too, and my friends will be safe.*

Just as she was about to give up hope that her idea had been anything other than madness, she hit the surface of the water with a stinging splash!

Suddenly, it was like the water opened around her, and

the world spun upside down. She was no longer falling down the well, but falling *up* it toward the sky. She was bone dry when she climbed from the well again to stand on solid ground beside it.

And there she stood, looking at a blinking frog and—somewhat weirder—at herself.

Not a person dressed up as her, but actually herself, in the outfit she'd worn the day she first met the frog prince.

She'd arrived in a fractured fairy tale.

"Um," said her duplicate.

"Yes, it's me," Rana told the shocked girl as calmly as she could. "Or I mean . . . I'm you, kind of. Hello."

"Um," the other her said again, which was disappointing. Rana'd hoped that, upon meeting herself for the first time, she'd have had more to say.

"We don't have a lot of time so I'll just explain," she told the girl and the frog in front of her. "You're characters in a fairy tale called 'The Frog Prince'—"

"Oh that's me!" said the frog cheerily.

"Yes," said Rana. "Well, you're a fractured version of the tale, although I don't quite know *how* fractured. By the looks of it, your version is not very different from my own.

Which will make this easier."

"Make what easier?" the other girl asked, glancing back over the edge of the well. "I lost my silver ball down the well and this frog was about to get it for me, if I agreed to marry him."

Rana frowned at the little frog. The frog shrugged. "I don't make the rules."

Rana rolled her eyes. "This isn't about your golden—er, I mean, silver—ball," she told herself. "And also, you should not agree to marry a frog just because he helps you get something you dropped."

"I wasn't *really* going to marry him!" said the other her.

"You *lied* to me, Princess Rana?" her frog prince objected. "Well, now I won't get your ball!"

"Listen to me," Rana told them. It was weird to be talking to another version of herself, but she carried on. "We don't have time to argue about balls. I need Prince Sebastian to go find his friend, Heinrich."

"How do you know about Heinrich?" the frog asked.

"The full title of this story is 'The Frog Prince or Iron Heinrich,' and, well, I need to find that Heinrich. We need him to... well, talk to himself. Show himself that he doesn't have to de-story everything to feel better. Do you know where he is?"

"He's probably waiting for me to meet the princess and fall in love," said the frog.

"So your story is almost like the original," said Rana.

"How do you know *this* isn't the original?" asked the other Rana, crossing her arms.

Rana found she couldn't explain. How *did* she know? She'd always assumed she was the original, but who could say when a story had been told and retold so many times? Maybe she was a fracture too. Maybe they all were, and there was no such thing as one original story. Maybe every version of a fairy tale was like the facet of a diamond, bending and reflecting the light in different ways, but none of them were the light itself.

"I don't know," Rana told her. "It doesn't really matter who's the original. I do know that we're all in danger if we can't show the Heinrich from my story that he *can* change."

"I'm afraid this doesn't make any sense to me," said the frog prince. Each of his frog eyes looked at the two Ranas separately, which was very disconcerting. "And now that I know you were deceiving me about marriage, I refuse to help you."

"But we need to—" Rana began to plead, though the frog prince cut her off with a wave of his little frog fist.

"I'd rather stay a frog forever than help two lying, scheming, selfish—"

He didn't get a chance to finish his list of unkind things, because the shadow had emerged from the well and passed through this story's frog prince on its way out.

The angry little frog gasped, turned gray, then white, then vanished.

"What happened?" the princess from the tale yelled.

"He's been de-storied!" Rana explained. "I'm so sorry, although I think you might be better off without that one. Now we have to run, or else we'll be de-storied too!"

The After looked puzzled at the both of them, then down at its two arms. It shrugged and stretched both arms out, one toward each princess.

Rana grabbed her double by the hand and yanked her away. They ducked around the shadow and ran to the other side of the well.

"Don't let it touch you," said Rana as she helped the other girl stand on the well's stone ledge.

"What are we doing?" the girl asked.

"We've got to go to another version of the story," Rana said. "We need a Heinrich whose heart isn't broken or one who's handling it a whole lot better."

"This is really weird," said the other Rana. "But whatever. It beats being bored. I'm in!"

Rana smiled. She couldn't imagine any version of herself that didn't like a reckless adventure.

As the After reached out across the opening of the well toward them, they jumped, twin princesses plummeting side by side into the dark.

They popped out together too, by another well, in another of their tales.

And beside a *third* princess. This one had a battle-axe on her back and a scar on her neck like she'd been beheaded and sewn back together. It looked *very* punk rock. Rana wanted to ask this version of herself all about her life and her stories, but the shadow rose from the well and came toward them. Relentless as ever.

"Who are you people?" this story's battle princess

demanded, raising her axe. "And what is *that*?"

"Don't let it touch you!" Rana warned the princess, but it was too late. She'd already attacked the After with her blade and sliced it right through the shadowy middle.

The axe turned to smoke in her hands, and then the After grabbed her and she vanished from existence too.

"No!" both Ranas yelled, and then jumped, once more hand in hand, back into the well, in search of yet another version of their tale, with no time to grieve or even think.

Another splash, another fall up another well, and they were out, standing in front of another frog prince and another Rana. This one had skin as dark and regal as Cinderella's, though the gown and the frog looked exactly the same. They both wore identical expressions of surprise.

"Pardon me?" said the princess. "And who might you two be?"

"I'm kind of in the middle of something," said the frog on the well beside her. He was holding a dripping-wet golden ball.

"Where is your friend Heinrich?" Rana asked as quickly as she could.

"Heinrich?" The frog jumped a little. "That brave soul! He

fought the witch who transformed me, and he perished in the process. I shall never forget him, and as soon as this princess becomes my bride, I will name our first child after him!"

"*When I what? You'll do what?*" this story's princess yelled at the frog prince. "Do I have a say in any of these plans?"

"Well . . . I . . . I was going to . . . I mean . . . ," the frog prince babbled. "I got your ball for you and I thought . . ."

"Think again!" the princess said and snatched the ball right out of the little frog's feet.

"Okay, well, good luck," said Rana as she turned back to the well to leave these two to whatever ending their story was going to have. "We have to keep searching."

"Wait!" this story's princess called after them. "Can I come with you?"

"What's your name?" Rana asked her.

"Oullie," the girl said. "Short for Grenouille." She looked down at her feet. "It means frog."

"Same!" said both Ranas at the same time.

"Of course you can come with us!" Rana said to Oullie. "Come on."

Before the After had even caught up with them in this

story, the three princesses jumped into the well.

"Not without me you don't!" Oullie's frog prince shouted and followed them.

After yet another fall through the darkness, three princesses and one frog splashed out from yet another well in the woods, all of them just as dry as ever (which in the frog's case was not very dry at all).

"Something terrible has happened here," said the frog prince immediately, surveying the scene.

"Oh get over it!" Rana scolded him. "You can't expect to plan a princess's whole life for her and not get so much as an argument from her. I'm telling you, I am sick of these princes who think even the slightest disagreement with them is some kind of terrible injustice, when really it's—"

"I think he's talking about this place," Oullie interrupted and pointed at the woods where they'd arrived.

The trees of the deep, dark wood weren't so much trees as they were charred and blackened stumps. There was no frog, nor another princess. The well was in ruins and the sky above was a hazy and unnatural red. They heard strange roars in the distance. Thundering steps shook the ground.

"I don't think we'll find help here," said Rana's double.

"What kind of help are we looking for?" asked Oullie. "What are y'all running from?"

Before anyone could explain about Heinrich and hearts that couldn't heal and the nature of the void, a giant robot burst through the burned and burning tree trunks.

The robot looked like a huge metal toad covered in spikes and laser cannons. Another Rana twin was in the driver's seat and a frog was strapped to her chest in a little harness with a little headset on. Two laser cannons aimed at Rana and her new friends.

"**Identify yourselves or be vaporized!**" clanged a robotic voice over a speaker. The laser cannons warmed up.

"I'm . . ." Rana started. "We're—"

"Duck, princess!" The little frog jumped on Rana's head, knocking her back just as the lasers blasted a tree to sawdust and smoke behind her. When the haze cleared, there stood the After, puzzled, but unharmed.

"Don't shoot! We're *you*!" Rana yelled up at herself driving the robot. This story was *very* different from her own. "And we need help!"

Another laser blast went right through the shadow's body. The After drifted toward the robot.

"**It's me and my frog against the world! No one else can be trusted,**" the metallic voice said. "**Evacuate or be destroyed.**"

"I like that the princess and the frog are a team in *this* version!" Oullie's frog prince said.

"Hush or I leave you here," Oullie told him, but she still picked him up and carried him back to the well when Rana led them to jump.

The princesses and the frog jumped from tale to tale. Some were quite like Rana's own; some seemed very different. There were fractures where everyone spoke languages she didn't speak, and there were fractures where everyone was a puppet or an alien or a blob of colorful goo. But they couldn't find a Heinrich in any of them.

"What if the one following you has absorbed all the others?" said Oullie. "Like the pull of its emptiness crossed from story to story and world to world and there's no one left who can help you."

"I don't believe that," said Rana.

"Why not?" the other Rana asked.

"Because that would mean this is hopeless," she said. "And I don't believe in hopelessness. That is *not* how I roll."

"We can't run forever," her twin told her.

They caught their breath beside a quiet well in a quiet wood in what looked like a quiet version of the story. The princess and the frog from this story were dancing in a nearby clearing and hadn't noticed their guests yet.

"I can run for as long as it takes," Rana replied. She walked toward the dancing couple, waving her arms to get their attention and ask them about their version of Heinrich.

"What's happening here?" this story's princess gasped when she saw Rana.

"I can't explain it again." Rana shook her head. "Do you know where Heinrich is?"

"Who?" asked the little frog.

"Your servant," said Rana.

"My servant? I don't have a servant," said the frog.

Rana slumped. She was about to leave this story to seek out yet another when she noticed how this version of herself held the frog protectively against her chest. "Wait, do you love this little guy?" she asked.

"Excuse me?" This princess balked. "That's a *personal* question!"

"Well, you and I are the same person, kind of," said Rana. "You can tell me."

"I suppose . . ." The princess looked at the frog, who looked at her eagerly. "I suppose I do!" She smiled and the frog smiled back. Then she kissed him gently on the snout.

With a flash of light as bright as the sun, in front of the princess stood a prince, grinning from ear to ear.

"Oh," said the princess, startled. She was still holding his hands and she let them go.

"That's not Sebastian," said Rana. This prince didn't look anything like Prince Sebastian.

"Who?" asked the prince. "My name's Prince Stuart."

"Oh," the princess from this story said again. "Hi, Stuart. I'm the princess."

"I know," he said. "Do you have a name?"

"I . . . um . . . no?" she said. "I've always just been The Princess."

"I think that's a beautiful name, The Princess," said Stuart.

They both laughed and blushed and laughed again.

"Are all happily ever afters this awkward?" asked Oullie.

"No idea," said Rana. "I've never seen one before."

"What is *that*?" The Princess asked, spinning Prince Stuart around and pointing at the well.

Rana had hoped the transformation might have been enough to stop the After, but she wasn't so lucky. The After had emerged from the well and wasn't the least bit interested in Prince Stuart.

It turned toward Rana, certain of its direction. It stretched out its arms. Rana backed away, leading it in a wide circle so she and the others could get to the well again. Her hope began to falter. What if she had been wrong? What if there was no way for Heinrich to change his story?

"I'll save you, my princess!" yelled a frog, leaping from the well and landing right on the shadow, knocking it backward. The heroic frog looked back at her once, winked, and then faded to nothing.

"Prince Sebastian!" Rana yelled, shocked out of her stupor.

"Yes?" another frog said from the well beside her. She turned and saw him perched on the stone, looking serious. "We won't go down without a fight," he added, and flicked his frog tongue.

Suddenly, ten, then twenty, then thirty more frogs jumped from the well and perched, ready to attack.

The After froze.

"What are you all doing here?" Rana asked.

"We're princes," said one of the frogs. "Saving princesses is what we do!"

"But how did you know I needed help?" Rana marveled.

"I went back for them the moment you left," Skyler explained with a curtsy after hauling herself out of the well in a less-than-princess-y way. "I told them it was urgent. Every one of them followed without hesitation."

"That's what *princesses* do," said Cindy, climbing out of the well next. She helped Rosamund, Sirena, Charlie, and the rest of Rana's friends from school out behind her. Even the Einhorn brothers stumbled from the well, arms full of chips and cookies.

"We brought snacks," said Danny Einhorn. "But we ate all the Cool Ranch Tortilla Balls on the way."

Rana smiled at them all. "How did you find me?"

"We're friends," Sirena told her, looking around at the fairy-tale woods they'd climbed into and at the After hovering in the air in front of them. "We can always find each other."

"Also my brothers and I are magic," added Danny Einhorn. "Duh."

"I'm glad you're here, but you could be de-storied," said Rana. "It's dangerous."

"Friends help each other," said Rosamund. "Those are the rules."

Rana hugged her. Maybe it wasn't the punk-rock thing to do, but she'd never been happier to see her friends in all her life.

"That's a rule I can follow," she told them.

CHAPTER FIFTEEN
Iron Heinrich

"Defensive circle, go!" Cindy commanded, and immediately, the friends and the frogs formed a massive circle around Rana and Sebastian.

A breeze in the woods ruffled Rana's hair and rattled the branches. Leaves spiraled down, but the After was unmoved. It floated just off the ground. It was hard to stare at the After. It hurt her eyes and hurt her soul even worse. Looking at Heinrich too long felt like falling.

"Listen, Heinrich," Sebastian called from her shoulder. "I don't know what you understand or even hear when I talk to you, but I need you to know that I want to help. *All of us* want to help you. Everyone here cares about you." He looked around at the gathered friends and frogs. "Right?"

They murmured a mixture of *sure*s and *I guess*es and *huh*s? It wasn't the rousing show of support he'd been aiming for.

"*Right?*" he repeated.

"Yeah!" they all chimed in together.

"I don't think this is helping," Rana warned as the shadow started moving.

"If you want Rana, you'll have to go through me," Rosamund told it.

"All of us!" shouted the colony of frogs and the crowd of princesses.

The Einhorn brothers let out a belch, which shook the earth with a sonic "boom!" There was a flash of light, and the next instant they had turned into grand and glorious unicorns.

"Dude, that always feels so weird," said RB.

"I kinda like it," said Van. "It tingles."

"Can we focus, guys?" said Danny, and pointed his horn at the approaching shadow.

They blasted it with all the magical light their horns could blast, rainbow sparkles erupting with the strength of a firehose.

The shadow absorbed it all, slowed but not stopped.

"Well, this isn't going great," said Danny.

"That *always* works! What gives?" said RB.

"Well, we've never tried it on a shadowy abyss monster before," said Van. "Anyone got any other ideas?"

"Cindy?" asked Charlie, because Cindy usually had great ideas. The princess shook her head.

Rana wanted to cry. She was so grateful for her friends and so scared of what was about to happen to them. She wiped her eyes with her T-shirt and sniffled.

The sniffle turned into a sob, tears of happiness and gratitude that no matter how far she wandered, her friends would find their way to help her. Strangers would come to her aid too and to each other's. Maybe the After's grief and rage was strong, but Rana's community was strong too.

"Whatever happens next, know that I love you guys," she said.

"Us too?" asked the frogs.

"You too," she told them. "All of you."

There was another earthshaking "boom" and another flash of light that lit the forest bright as day. Everyone ducked and shielded their eyes. This wasn't unicorn magic though . . . this was a curse being lifted.

When Rana blinked her sight back, where once she'd

been surrounded by a colony of frogs, she now stood among a throng of princes. Some were identical, and some looked very different. One was not human at all, and four weren't even princes, but princesses themselves.

"Whoa," said Skyler, looking from one to the next with absolute awe on her face.

Except there was one frog left, sitting on Rana's shoulder. His chest fluttered and his tongue flicked. His eyes darted in every direction.

"Um . . . *what*?" the frog prince exclaimed. *"No!"* An incredulous frog could make a shocking amount of noise. Birds took flight and animals fled his angry croaking. "I'm the only frog left? Your love changed all of these other frogs from all these other stories, and not me! That's not fair!"

Rana looked back at the After. It had been repelled by the light, but not transformed and not destroyed. The creature was still a void shaped like a human and still in pursuit. Her heart sank. She thought she understood what had happened. It was her fault, in a way. "We fractured our story with everything we've done. My love isn't what can transform you anymore."

"*But then what can?*" Sebastian cried out.

"I have an idea!" Skyler rushed over to him. She leaned so close to Rana that for a moment she thought the girl was going to kiss *her*, but instead, Skyler planted a smooch right on the frog prince's snout. She closed her eyes, whispered, "I love you," and counted to three.

Rana braced herself to have a fully grown human prince on her shoulder.

But there was no flash of light. No transformation.

"Were you *faking* it?" Rana asked.

Skyler shook her head. "Not a bit. I really do love him! I think? I mean . . . who can say? I've never been in love with a frog prince before. It feels a little like being sick, but like being sick on a really fun roller coaster?"

A murmur of agreement passed through some of the princes and princesses. "Yeah, that's what it feels like."

The frog prince groaned. "We've tried everything!"

The After reached out toward Rana and Sebastian on her shoulder.

We haven't tried everything, Rana realized.

"She's not from our story," said Rana. "None of them are.

Quick, everyone, out of the way. Now!"

"What?" they asked, but Rana started pushing them aside so they didn't get in the After's path of desolation.

"Do you trust me?" she asked the frog prince.

"Um . . . yeah?"

"That wasn't totally convincing."

"Well, I'd love to hear your plan first," he said.

"Heinrich's pain is a part of his story. A part of . . ." She looked between the frog prince on her shoulder and the shadow that was Heinrich. "*Your story*," she said. "It can't be solved by running away. It has to be solved by—"

"Going to him," said the frog prince.

"I think *he* is your destiny," said Rana. "I think the love story in 'The Frog Prince' is about friendship. *Your* friendship with Heinrich. That's the love that makes a happily ever after."

"Rana, not to yuck your idea here," Charlie said, "but the guy is literally a monster. How's Sebastian supposed to love him?"

Rana shrugged. "Maybe the only one who can turn you human is the one who needs you to turn him human too."

"That's a way better description of love than being sick on a roller coaster," Sirena noted. "The people we love make us human."

"So true," added Bea, who had some experience with this kind of thing herself.

"But I'm scared," said the frog prince, looking at the long arms of the shadow. "What if it doesn't work and he de-stories me? What if he can't forgive how I abandoned him?"

"You have to try," said Rana. "We can't outrun him forever. Trying even when you're scared is what makes it brave. Trying when the danger's real is what makes it heroic. Real happy endings don't just happen automatically. Heroes make them happen."

"I'm still just a frog," he said.

"A frog can be a hero," Rana told him. "If he acts like one."

The frog nodded and puffed his little frog chest and spoke to the shadow. "Heinrich, if you can hear me ... um ... I'm sorry."

The shadow stopped. Everyone froze and hung on the frog prince's words. Rana felt his webbed feet shift nervously on her shoulder. "Keep going," she whispered.

"I'm sorry I left without saying goodbye," said the prince. "I shouldn't have left you behind to run off after some random princess."

"I mean, I'm not just some random princess," Rana muttered to herself.

"There's so much I want to tell you," Sebastian told the After. "All about Oreos and Cool Ranch Tortilla Balls and no-teams basketball and boarding school and fractured fairy tales. But our story is called the 'The Frog Prince or Iron Heinrich.' I can't have a story without you. I miss you, buddy."

The shadow flickered. It wavered. For a moment, Rana thought she saw some light coming through it, escaping it like a star bursting out of a black hole.

The frog hopped down from Rana's shoulder and did an amazingly brave thing. He hopped up to the shadow and sat before it, looking into its depths. And then he raised one froggy foot toward it.

"Careful!" Rana warned. She'd suggested this idea but didn't think the frog would risk annihilating himself because of it.

The frog prince looked back at her. "Don't worry," he

said. "I trust you, but I also trust him, my loyal Heinrich, whose heart is stronger than iron."

He hopped as high as he could and touched the shadow before the shadow could touch him.

The forest echoed with a sudden "CLANG!"

Everyone startled. Even the frog prince jumped backward.

The shadow flickered.

A second "CLANG" made Rana's eardrums ring.

"*Too loud!*" the Einhorn brothers all whinnied. They turned themselves back into boys so they could crouch down and cover their ears. Unicorns don't like loud noises unless they're the ones making them.

A third "CLANG" shook the world. It was so loud that everyone fell to their knees and squeezed their eyes shut.

But when Rana dared open one eye and then the other, she saw something remarkable.

Standing in a shower of leaves shaken loose from the trees stood a boy, about their age, with ruddy cheeks and messy red hair, wearing the livery of a castle servant, a bit worse for wear, but no dirtier than the rest of them by the well in the woods.

At his feet lay three iron bands, broken.

"Heinrich?" the frog prince croaked.

The boy had tears in his eyes. "I'm saved!" he cried out and scooped the little frog up into his fully human hands. "You saved me! After everything I did, you *still* saved me! I can't believe it."

"Of course I did," said the frog prince. "You're my friend."

The boy's smile was as bright as his shadow had been dark.

"But I couldn't have done it without these friends," said the frog prince, looking back at Rana and the other princes and princesses.

"They all cared enough to risk their lives for each other, and for us, a shadow and a frog!" Heinrich marveled. "What luck to have found them!"

"Yeah, I guess," said Prince Sebastian. "I'm a pretty lucky frog."

There was no "CLANG," nor a flash of light. It was more like a blink. Where one moment Rana had been looking at a frog talking to a servant, she was now looking at Prince Sebastian, a human boy, maybe a little greener than he had been before, but restored to himself.

Sebastian's eyes went wide. He ran his hands over his chest, his legs, the top of his head. Then he spun around. "Am I—? Is this—?"

"You're you again," said Rana. "A lot less portable."

"Woo-hoo!" The prince jumped for joy and embraced his servant in a long hug. "I'm me!"

Rana watched them with a smile, glad Sebastian had finally seen that friends could be his destiny as much as any princess, and that Heinrich had seen, well . . . she had no idea what he'd learned, but it didn't matter. He was restored and the peril was passed.

"Let's go home," Sebastian suggested to his servant, clapping his hand around the redheaded boy's shoulder. "We have a lot to catch up on."

They turned toward the well when a loud throat clearing stopped them.

"What about us?" asked one the of the princes who had been a frog in a different tale.

"Yeah!" said another. "He de-storied our princesses! We've got nothing to go back to!"

"You're all human now," said Rana. "You don't need a princess to *make* you human. You can make your own story happen for yourselves."

"But what are we supposed to *do*?" another one asked.

"I have an idea," said Bea with a smile. "You ever think about going to school?"

At her invitation, a door appeared in the space between two trees, hovering in the air, like the magic had been waiting for just the right opportunity to show itself.

On the other side of the door in the air, the gates of the Academy stood open. The real world. Madame Phoebe stood beside the gates, like she'd been expecting the door to open all along.

In fact, she tapped her wristwatch. "Well, *that* took long enough," she grumbled. "Cold lunch in the cafeteria today. I let Professor Perrault eat all the hot mac 'n' cheese Tater Tots."

The princes looked at each other and Rana winked at Bea. A few dozen new princes at the Academy would definitely solve the boy-girl ratio problem.

"Do I have to go back too?" Skyler asked nervously.

Rana shrugged. "We make our own rules. What do you want to do?"

Skyler looked at Prince Sebastian, who blushed. "It's

"'The Frog Prince *or* Iron Heinrich,'" Sebastian reminded her and turned to Heinrich. "What do you say, Heinrich? How about adding a new princess to our tale?"

Heinrich smiled and gave him a little nod. Skyler grinned from ear to ear as the boys extended their hands together to invite Skyler along, the newest fairy-tale princess, by way of an amusement park.

"Well, what about you?" Cindy asked Rana.

Rana looked from her friends and the doorway back to school and the world she longed for, and to the well that led back to her tale. She took a deep breath.

"I have to take care of something that I can't do from outside my story," she said. "Something important."

"Is it a witch?" asked Charlie.

"Or a curse?" asked Rosamund.

"Or another prince?" asked Sirena.

Rana shook her head. "It's what I've been running from all along," she told them. "My parents."

CHAPTER SIXTEEN
A New Princess

Skyler and Prince Sebastian held hands on the way back to the castle, while Heinrich walked beside them, listening to all the things Prince Sebastian had learned about the world beyond the fairy tale.

"Wait, what? The *earth* rotates?" Heinrich cried out. "Are you saying the earth is . . . *round*?" His mouth hung open like a doorway to another world.

"Oh, buddy, just wait until I tell you what pizza is!" Prince Sebastian said, leading Heinrich forward again.

Rana trotted ahead to the front steps of her parents' castle, but on the threshold, she hesitated. She was still dressed in the black jeans and torn-up T-shirt she had been wearing when her parents had last seen her, although now the outfit was much dirtier. What would they say to her? What would they think of her when she told them what she wanted to do, what she wanted to *be*?

Before she knew it, Prince Sebastian and Skyler stood on either side, offering support.

"You got this," said Prince Sebastian. "Just tell them the truth."

She took a deep breath and entered the castle to find her parents seated in the throne room, as if they'd been expecting to receive visitors.

Of course they'd be here, thought Rana. *Because this is the most dramatic place for me to meet them.* Stories had their own rules.

She curtsied after making her approach below the dais where they sat, just as she had been taught a perfect princess should. Skyler did the same, while Sebastian and Heinrich each offered a formal bow with one hand behind his back. Everyone, so far, played their part.

"May we have some privacy, dear Father?" Rana asked as sweetly as she could. Her father dismissed the servants, although Heinrich remained with Prince Sebastian, unwilling to leave his friend so soon after their reunion.

The moment the last of the royal servants left, Rana's mother addressed her with dismay. "I see you remain adorned in a most unprincess-like fashion."

"This is quite shocking, my darling!" her father exclaimed. "You do not look at all like yourself. I fear a changeling is in our midst!"

"I'm not a changeling, Father," she told him. "I'm me. I'm more me, in fact, than you have ever seen before. I'm sorry that's upsetting to you."

Her parents gave her long looks that were not so much disapproving as they were utterly perplexed.

"I am utterly perplexed," her father said.

"I don't mean to perplex you," said Rana. "But I've had a long few days now and haven't slept much, so excuse me if I'm a little abrupt. I'm tired, and I'm hungry, and I'm sure I don't smell great."

"You definitely don't," whispered Prince Sebastian, but Skyler and Heinrich elbowed him.

"I am not the perfect princess you want me to be," Rana told her parents. "I don't think anyone *could* be, but especially not me. I don't want to be spoiled or treated like a fragile doll. And I don't want to marry a prince or even to stay here in the castle. I want to go back to school."

"I'm sorry, darling." The queen leaned forward, tilting her head. "I don't believe I heard you properly."

"You heard me," said Rana. "I think you heard all of it."

Her parents looked at one another again, and then back at her.

"Are you under some kind of spell?" her father asked. "Because there are witches in this world who can do terrible things. If a witch has ensorcelled you, we can call upon an un-ensorceller at once!"

"I'm not under a witch's spell," said Rana. "I broke the witch's wand."

Her mother gasped. "You did *what*?"

"It's a long story," she said. "And it was scary, and dangerous, and strange, but it was also kind of awesome. To be honest, I love having adventures and getting messy and standing shoulder to shoulder with my sisters and brothers in the face of strange perils. I don't *like* being safe and quiet and bored all the time. I *like* taking risks and being loud and sometimes even being wrong."

Her mother dropped her head into her hands in a great show of lamentation. "What has happened to our perfect Princess Rana?"

Rana left her friends and climbed onto the dais, like it

was the stage back at school. She knelt between her parents and took their hands in hers. "I am still Rana, but I was never perfect. No one is. I want to go to school, and I want to play really loud music, and I want to be with my friends. I want to make my own story, and I'd like to do it with your blessing."

"But . . ." Her father burst into tears. He even let out a little snot bubble, which was not a very kingly thing to do, and which made all three of them laugh. Rana felt her own tears falling.

"I am not sure I am made to handle any of this," said her mother. "It's per—"

"Perplexing, I know," said Rana, still holding their hands. "The world isn't some golden ball to be admired. It's meant to be tossed, and turned, and dirtied, and dropped sometimes. It's not supposed to be perfect, even though it can be beautiful. It can also be sad and angry and silly and strange. It's *meant* to be perplexing. That's what keeps it interesting."

"I'm not sure *we* are supposed to be interesting," said the king.

"I've seen enough fractured fairy tales to know that

we're all interesting," she said. "If we let ourselves be."

Her parents sniffled. Her mother gave her father a handkerchief.

"You said you go to school?" she asked Rana. "And you like being wrong about things?"

"Sounds dreadful," muttered the king.

"Maybe it is," said Rana, with another squeeze of her father's fingers. "But the snacks are good."

"Is this what you truly want?" her mother asked. "A different world than ours?"

Rana nodded.

"Can we come visit?" the king asked in almost a whisper.

Rana nodded again. "Of course," she said. "I'd insist on it."

"Well." Her father cleared his throat and stood in his proclamation-making pose. He clapped twice and the servants came shuffling back into the room. "It is then decreed that Princess Rana shall continue her studies in the—"

"The real world," Rana whispered.

"The real world!" the king declared.

Rana smiled. It turned out, the conversation she'd been avoiding for ages hadn't been so hard after all. She just had to travel between a few worlds, battle a witch, face down a hungry shadow, and help a frog become a human to get ready for it.

"Why don't you two come with me now?" she asked her parents. "You can take me back to school and meet my friends and teachers and our headmistress. You'll see, I'm in good hands, even if they aren't anything like you'd imagined for me."

"And you can perform your music for us when we visit," said her mother.

"I . . ." She didn't want to say no, but she was pretty sure they wouldn't like punk rock. Then again, they didn't have to like it. She was just happy they wanted to hear it. "I'd love that," she told them. "It is kind of loud though."

"Fetch the royal earplugs!" her father commanded. "And pack our royal bags!"

CHAPTER SEVENTEEN
The Start of Something

At first, Madame Phoebe was shocked to see the king and queen from Rana's tale arrive at the gates to the Academy.

After the shock, however, came an idea that delighted her.

"We'll host a parents' weekend," said the fairy godmother turned headmistress. "It will give me an opportunity to do one real-world activity we've never done at the HEA before!"

"What's that?" Cindy wondered.

"Ask for donations," said Madame Phoebe. "Heaven knows keeping this place running on magic alone is exhausting. We need some money."

And just like that, with the headmistress's grumpy decree, a new tradition began.

"I don't think I'll be inviting my wicked stepmother," Cindy said.

"Or your stepsisters," Charlie reminded her. They both

shuddered. Back in her tale, her wicked stepfamily had met a terrible and gruesome fate.

"I hope my father will come!" Sirena cheered.

"Mine too," said Bea. "Although he's a humble inventor; he doesn't have much money to give the school."

"Of course," said Madame Phoebe. "All orphans or peasants or princesses with evil parents are exempt from extending invitations to parents' weekend." She cleared her throat. "The rest better cough up some gold."

On the big day, a surprising number of fairy-tale parents had come. They were dazzled by electricity, alarmed by the fashions, and as delighted to discover the variety of snack foods the real world offered as their children had been. Even the old sea king, Sirena's father, found himself stuffing his face with tortilla chips.

"Nothing stays crunchy under the sea," he mumbled with his mouth full. "This is spectacular! Better than krill!"

As the royal parents munched on snacks, Rana stood backstage, pacing and biting her nails. Her golden guitar sat in its stand, ready to rock.

"Relax, you know you've got this!" Rosamund reassured her, strapping on a bass guitar. Cindy stood to the side, drumsticks in hand, a fierce and focused look on her face. She was rehearsing their song one more time in her head. Cindy stayed a perfectionist, no matter how many times Rana had explained punk rock didn't need to be perfect. In fact, perfection was the enemy of punk.

"Listen, if I'm going to be in your band and play this 'music,' then I'm going to do it my way," Cindy had told her. Rana let her dig at the music slide. If being in a band with her friends meant compromising a little, then that's what she'd do. This was about to be their first gig, and the first time any of their families had heard this kind of music.

"Everyone's ready," Sirena said, rushing backstage to fix her makeup for the show. She'd offered to be a backup singer, but told Rana it was Rana's band, and her song, so *she* had to be the lead singer.

"You might not have been the main character in your fairy tale," Sirena had explained. "But you are going to be the main character in this band."

"Rana and the Rebel Princesses," said Rosamund.

"We decided already," said Cindy. "So don't argue."

Rana felt like she could cry from happiness, but instead

she did the least punk thing imaginable: she gave everyone a hug.

On the stage, Madame Phoebe was giving a short speech. "We're grateful to all of you royal parents for being here today. I know it is not easy when your daughters and sons decide to leave the stories you've built for them to seek out their own happily ever afters, but I promise you, in the Princess Protection Program, we are giving them the tools they'll need for whatever adventures await them. As long as you turn over some of your treasure. Snacks aren't free, you know? And now, with apologies and a promise that I had nothing to do with it, I present to you what the youth are calling: music."

"We're on," Cindy whispered, and nudged Rana forward onto the stage. Her band followed behind her.

"Whoa," Rana whispered, looking at the crowd that had gathered to watch the performance.

The whole school was there, all the princesses from all the tales from all over the world. The fractured frog princes were there too, and the unicorn triplets, and Charlie and his friend Royal, wayward princes themselves, and then there were the parents, every shade of royalty imaginable, looking expectant, looking confused. And right in the center, Rana's mom and dad, the king and queen, among a throng of kings and queens, looking hopeful and nervous in equal measure.

Rana cleared her throat into the mic. A squelch of feedback made her flinch. "Sorry," she muttered. "Um . . . this is a song I wrote after my last adventure. It's called 'After Ever After,' and it's . . . well . . ." She smiled as she got her hands into position on the guitar. "Mom and Dad, this one's for you. Thanks for crossing worlds to meet me here." She took a deep breath, looked at Cindy on the drums, and nodded.

Cindy tapped out the beat on her drumsticks. "A one and a two and a one-two-three-four!"

Rana, the punk-rock princess, erupted with the song she'd always dreamed of singing, loud and proud in front of every person that mattered to her, and none of them had ever heard anything like it before.

And she was just getting started.